THE HAND OF WILLOW'S END

BY:

BENNARD TERRELL

TABLE OF CONTENTS

I should have left it alone; should have locked up that room forever and thrown away key to seal off what was about to be unleashed upon world but instead found myself compelled toward glass case in which rested this thing no longer living nor yet quite dead either. There being no lock on it whatsoever save for a simple latch holding lid shut tight – clicked softly when opened, I knew these acts were wrong.

Touching the hand caused mansion to exhale deeply through every window pane at once; icy gusts of wind rushed past my face carrying with them sheets of paper fluttering anxiously like frightened birds desperate for escape before being sucked into nothingness beyond walls around me forevermore. Fingers recoiled from contact as though burned by some unseen flame within those cold dead limbs; slamming down cover over top again whereat everything went silent excepting my own heartbeat pounding against eardrums until too late had already occurred.

That night sleep brought forth nightmares – visions filled with crawling spiders made from human hands palest white imaginable moving across dark floors lined by heavy drapes leaving trails behind them smeared blackness deeper than any nightshade could ever produce even under moonless sky. Each one ending same way too: feeling thin fingers tighten around throat until awakened gasping for breath unable to speak or move for several minutes afterwards due fright experienced during such an event taking place only moments prior while unconscious mind still gripped tightly onto consciousness left behind like claw marks scraped along innermost recesses where they never belonged in first instance anyway.

Next morning came light – empty glass case where hand used to rest stared back emptily into dimly lit room around it where once there had been something beautiful now only absence remained like void within oneself after losing something important forever; sound heard then was worst ever known to humanity – slow dragging scrape followed by sharp thud against wood board floor coming from deep inside mansion.

I knew then that I was not alone. The hand had a life of its own and it wanted nothing good for those who called Willow's End their home.

The noise stopped as soon as it had begun, and the house became quiet again. I was motionless with my mind racing. The logical part of my brain, which dismissed ghosts and ghouls as mere tales for children around a campfire, tried to rationalize all that was happening before me now; but the primitive instinct inside knew perfectly well what this meant – I was in danger.

I took a deep breath and decided to explore the mansion. If I were going spend another night under its roof then there was no way around it; I had to know what was going on here! Sensible thoughts like fleeing crossed my mind but curiosity of an author who wants to know every single detail about their story stopped me from moving anywhere else plus outside didn't seem any better with raging storm.

In one of those dusty rooms off some creaky hallway (there seemed be many such places) where history still lingered heavily around each corner waiting just beyond perception's reach- that's when things got really creepy: portraits watched us move, books talked gibberish at us though we couldn't understand word they said, furniture covered up like ghosts lying in wait for someone passing by.

As I went deeper into this building which seemed larger on inside than out indicated by its exterior appearance alone would suggest even if including numerous wings stretching away from main structure along different axes through webs of hallways lined mostly with dust that made footfalls echo -a very ominous sign-, something inside me started feeling more uneasy with every step taken further inward through these seemingly endless corridors filled only by silence broken occasionally either by distant howling wind or screeching floorboard somewhere nearby. Storms may cause noises too though so told myself it must have been just another trick played upon minds scared silly half to death already yet incapable thinking straight anymore having lost touch reality completely given circumstances faced thus far.

Then there came a time when my imagination failed keeping up pace and I couldn't think of anything new anymore. The ground floor was huge; it had many rooms leading off from corridors that groaned with every step. Every room told a story – old portraits stared down at me as if they knew something I didn't, books whispered strange words in languages too foreign for my mind to comprehend (or maybe it was just gibberish), dusty furniture wrapped up in white sheets like abandoned bodies waiting for their souls to return.

But the further I went into this place, the more scared I became. It got colder and darker, especially around corners where shadows seemed thicker than elsewhere or when storm outside unleashed its fury upon windows causing panes rattle against frame; then there were times when wind howled through keyholes like creature writhing pain somewhere beyond hearing range but close enough make hair stand end on arms anyway even though should have been used by now being so deep within bowels haunted house such as this one...

And that's when things started getting really strange indeed: because just before me now stood a staircase which spiraled downwards into absolute blackness! Basement most likely? Yes, definitely so since scraping sound came from below somewhere near these steps must lead thereabouts somewhere beneath us both- but how far down did they go exactly? Only way find out would be take first step forward into unknown territory where no light yet reached nor ever could reach unless brought along myself somehow thus revealing dark secrets concealed beneath surface layer of normal everyday life!

The flame spread with haste. The dried vegetation fueled the fire, creating a ring of fire around the hand in no time. It twitched a second time, then more violently before it started dragging itself towards the edge of the altar, towards me.

I backed off; my feet tripping over themselves as I went and watched as it fell to the floor and began to crawl towards me with its fingers moving like a spider's legs — a truly horrifying spectacle. It was coming for me: driven by some kind of insatiable longing.

And so I ran. Through darkness, upstairs, past thundering breaths trapped louder than lightening in my ears until I was back into the library where safety echoed silence off every book cover there ever was. Slamming doors shut behind us seemed less important now but I still did it anyway before leaning against cold wood that had never been warmer than this moment right here…

Leaning against that door frame while listening out for any sign of pursuit or approach but all there is just wind howling outside mixed up with my ragged breathing which sounds like relief because for now at least We Are Safe weren't we? But even though we might have been safe then I knew from that point on — from this moment forward — until things change one day soon enough do change again oh yes indeed, they will surely have no other choice but to keep changing over & over & over again…

CHAPTER 2:

The First Night

While barricading myself into the library, the wind outside howled with anger almost like my racing heart. It seemed that this was not going to be a nightmare of a first night in the Ashcroft mansion and each groan of that old house only made me fear more. However tired I felt at that moment, sleep was not anywhere close – all because I had let out a crawling cut-off hand by mistake.

The library became my refuge; its book-filled walls gave me some solace against the madness even though they did not speak. To increase lighting, I took away a heavy desk lamp and to hold up my flimsy barrier several thick volumes. My hands moved over the books' spines as if searching for something else to think about but there was nothing else on my mind except an image of an evil living hand.

When it grew closer to midnight, so did the storm: lightning flashed across skies while slamming rain onto windows which looked like they could break any moment from such battering ramming winds outside them. During those brief flashes everything around seemed still as shadows danced grotesquely at their edges most likely due to their own movements being momentarily revealed by those sharp lights.

Along with those eerie noises coming from every part of this mansion as if it were complaining about being attacked by such weather – any one of which could easily cover up sounds made by stealthily moving severed limbs – what occurred next inside my head? Of course! Ideas about it climbing walls with its fingers or creeping overhead across ceilings waiting until now when least expected… Then again maybe during another gust… Come on! How much longer can we breathe here?

I couldn't stay defenseless against some unknown menace like a sitting duck; therefore, having made up mind, I moved forward readying oneself for anything. Ridiculousness passed through me although picked sturdy candlestick rather than anything capable of warding off an attack (which was funny given what I expected). But before stepping out, taking deep breaths helped to calm down – otherwise nerves would have gone into overdrive.

There was such a mess in the room, the furniture toppled over, and the wallpaper like dead skin peeled off of it. Right there among all that chaos was a hand. It clawed at the wooden floor with fervor. Deep grooves were carved into the wood as if it had been looking for something buried beneath.

I couldn't move as I watched it move intelligently for what shouldn't have been disturbing intelligence, digging and scrapping with its fingers. Then, after sensing me somehow, it stopped. Slowly, it turned around; its fingers twisted unnaturally to point in my direction.

In panic I swung down with all my might on the hand with a candlestick. There was a sickening crunch throughout the room followed by high pitched shrieking sound that seemed to be coming from within walls themselves. The hand twitched violently then went still.

For a moment relief washed over me until I realized shrieking had not stopped; if anything, it grew louder and more anguished – no human throat could produce such a sound. Walls began vibrating under intensity of scream plaster cracking like mansion itself is in pain.

Screams chased me down hallway spurring me on in blind rush to escape until I reached library slamming door behind me collapsing against it breathless trembling.

While sitting there on cold floor screams eventually subsided but mansion was different now there was malevolence in air presence that hadn’t been there before as if by striking hand i’d woken up something much worse.

The storm outside continued unabated indifferent to horrors taking place inside Ashcroft mansion and i knew one thing with chilling certainty: nightmare has only just begun

The book was called "Secret Ceremonies and Cults of New England." I opened it with a sense of dread mixed with urgency. The pages were filled with careful penmanship, noting various supernatural incidents and dark rituals that had reportedly taken place in the New England area. It didn't take me long to find the section on Willow's End, and specifically, the Ashcroft family.

According to the text, the Ashcrofts were heavily involved in occultism; they pursued eternal life and power through forbidden means. A margin note written in shaky handwriting said that the severed hand was believed to be Silas Ashcroft's -- Silas being the sorcerer patriarch who first built the mansion. He had met a violent end at the hands of his own followers during some unsuccessful ceremony where his hand got cut off.

While I was getting my head around this less than cheery past, an idea started forming. If that thing was Silas Ashcroft's hand, maybe it was still attached to his spirit or whatever scraps of it hung around in this house. Destroying it could break that connection – give peace to my surroundings and myself a chance at safety.

But as I planned, the estate seemed to react. The wind picked up outside, howling through cracks like it was trying to scream its way indoors. And just like that, the air turned icier by several degrees; I watched my breath come out in front of me as if suddenly standing outside on a winter night. Then something new joined in with storm's lament: a soft dragging thump... thump... thump which grew louder all time closer.

It came from down library hallway. I blew out lamp quickly so room went black – except for when lightning would flash outside and briefly illuminate window panes – then dove behind one big reading chair across from door while keeping eyes glued on library exit.

Finally thumping halted; we shared tense silence for what felt like minutes long. And then, out of nowhere, door handle began to turn itself slowly. Door groaned open wider until it showed nothing but darkness stretching on into rest of hallway – but I knew it wasn't empty. Presence could be felt, taste was thick on tongue – suffocating air.

Suddenly candlestick seemed such a small weapon in my hand. Wider still door swung, and strong gust cold blew right past me into room; with this came smell rot so strong it felt like would never leave nose once it got there. And framed by that doorway during momentary flash caused by another lightning strike was hand sitting there like some awful spider perched on ledge with fingers starting twitch.

More than just hand became visible during that bolt its light: behind it loomed shadow, shape large and imposing but indistinct – watcher dark who kept eye upon minion's deeds.

Lightning ceased. Room went black again. Hand started moving forward now, dragging body along floor so cloth scraped softly over wood. I held onto candlestick tight as I realized that confrontation was inevitable... next move could easily be my last.

CHAPTER 3:

Town Secrets

Timid dawn peeped through the shattered windows of the mansion, prompting me to go outside. I was tired in body and mind after a night of nightmares, but sleep had not touched me. The storm was over; it had left behind an oppressive silence that hung over Willow's End like the whole town was holding its breath. I decided to talk to the locals and see if I could find out more about the Ashcroft legacy, maybe even make a friend in this nightmare.

Willow's End was one of those small towns where news travels faster than wind. As I walked along its streets, damp from last night's rain, I saw evidence of the storm's fury: branches down and debris in the roads. The few people I met cast wary glances my way; not just distrust of an unfamiliar face but something deeper – an inherited wariness of anything connected with the Ashcroft mansion.

I found my way to a local diner – a squat brick building that looked like it had weathered many storms -- and went inside. The smell of hot coffee and fried bacon did little to calm me down. I sat at the counter and ordered coffee for myself while eavesdropping on conversations around me.

“It’s him – the one who moved into Ashcroft’s place,” said an old woman in hushed tones to her companion, curiosity mixing with suspicion in her voice.

“Yeah, word got ‘round,” replied another woman, casting a glance at me before quickly looking away. “Martha’s boy saw him last night… wandering about like one them Ashcroft ghosts.”

Their words confirmed what already seemed obvious: around here, ‘Ashcroft’ is synonymous with ‘bad luck.’ Needing specifics, I turned to the waitress refilling my cup.

“I heard this place has some history with that old Ashcroft mansion,” I said casually. “I’m staying there for a while.”

She paused for a moment, her face tightening. “Mister, I’d advise you not to stick around long. That place… it’s got a bad history. Bad blood and worse spirits. Most of us keep clear of it.”

“Why?” I pressed, feeling that her reluctance stemmed from more than just fear.

She sighed and glanced around before leaning in closer. "Look, we don't talk about it much no more. But folks say Silas Ashcroft meddled with things no man should've touched. Darkness that didn't die with him neither. Every couple year's something terrible happens 'round there – people see things; people disappear."

Her words were discouraging but not enough to make me abandon my quest for knowledge. I thanked her and left a generous tip before heading off to the next stop on my list: the local library might have public records, old newspapers or books which could shed some light on these cryptic comments.

The library was an ancient stone building covered with ivy that stood at the edge of town like an old sentinel. Inside was quiet – so quiet you could hear the rustle of each page being turned in a book across the room. The librarian, an elderly man with spectacles sliding down his nose, watched me curiously as I approached.

"I'm researching the history of the Ashcroft mansion," I said, affecting an academic tone of voice as best I could.

He took a moment to examine me before giving a slow nod. "We've got some old newspapers and local genealogies in the archives that you might find interesting." He walked me over to a corner of the library, where stacks of leather-bound volumes and yellowing papers teetered.

I went through the stuff for hours. It was like the dark history of this town was jumping right off the pages: unexplained deaths, disappearances, witchcraft — you name it. One article from 1924 caught my eye. It detailed a grisly scene in which an area family had been found slaughtered, their bodies marked with what were called "occult" symbols. The case went unsolved, but rumors pointed to the last surviving member of the Ashcroft family, who disappeared shortly before the murders.

As I read on about these bone-chilling accounts, a shadow fell across the page. I glanced up and saw a man standing there, his face hard and his eyes cold.

"You shouldn't dig too deep," he said in a low voice that sounded anything but friendly. "Some things are better left buried."

And with that he spun around and walked away, leaving me alone with his words hanging in the air like fog. I gathered up my photocopies and hurried back to the mansion — shaken not so much by what he'd said as by how much it resembled every clichéd horror movie ever made — but little did I know that night in that house would be only the beginning; no sirree! Little did I know that all hell was about to break loose at this place.

CHAPTER 4:

Vanishing

This chapter begins with a mysterious encounter at the library, making the journey back home to the mansion feel longer and colder than ever before. It was getting cloudy again. There were dark grey clouds that seemed to sit on top of Willow's End like a lead blanket. The air felt alive, electric–like there might be thunder not just above me but beneath my feet.

Walking up to the house, I pushed open the gate which creaked ominously behind me. It was an eerie sound; one that I'd grown oddly used to over the years. But it always made my skin crawl when it followed me down the lane like this… when it echoed in my ears for more than a few seconds.

I stopped.

The wind blew through the trees and whispered in my ear… and carried with it a low, mournful moan that had not been there before now. A child's cry from far off…

Looking back towards the house one last time, I saw something strange—a hand print? A small imprint left in wet earth; leading from where I stood up into woods bordering our property.

The touch sent a shiver through me.

It wasn't confined to these four walls anymore…

Fearful of what could be lurking out there (and filled with enough guilt about everything else), I decided to follow them — grabbing my flashlight and candlestick as usual before heading out into those woods.

I have no idea what had come over me at this point… or why any sane person would decide this was a good idea alone… but there you have it.

Stepping past town line signpost, I entered an eerie world barely lit by moonlight above – only able to see about ten yards ahead thanks mostly due heavy rain last night. Trees lined road either side taller first mile or so then giving way lower shrubs closer we got entrance proper woodlands themselves starting show signs civilization encroaching upon them.

The trail was still there — leading deeper into the forest but marks more erratic now (like creature had gotten… excited? Agitated?) My heart pounded in my ears as I pushed through bushes and brambles with no regard for what might be lurking just out of sight either side. It really didn't matter at this point though, did it? Nothing mattered anymore…

I entered clearing next to stream bed about hour later when suddenly – everything stopped. The wind stopped. The trees stopped moving. Even rain above seemed hold its breath long enough give me clear view forest around us.

There wasn't much see.

It was a small area – maybe fifteen twenty feet across at widest point — but ground disturbed here like something had dug itself into frenzy. Dirt everywhere. Sticks broken half roots pulled up from earth like masses worms wriggling free light day after flood rains last year.

Shining flashlight around, my eyes fell on something that made blood freeze cold veins:

Partially hidden beneath one those bushes… was child's shoe.

My heart skipped beat I went pull back jacket sleeve check phone screen again time before trusting what seeing front me. But there was no denying it: brown leather finish; frayed laces stained dark dried blood; too small fit anyone older than ten years old most likely…

Something behind tree caught eye then – white fabric flapping gently wind coming off riverbed nearby… A piece shirt maybe? Ragged edges looked soaked through with same rusty colored hue found all over other clothes left behind by previous victims fallen prey madman who haunted these woods since before even mansion itself built atop his grave…

I had seen enough movies know how this ends…

But if felt different now somehow… closer home than ever before perhaps?

This thing wasn't some dumb slasher flick monster chasing down teenagers lost their way through forbidden forest on prom night only kill them while they fuck each other silly next abandoned cabin backwoods…

This was real.

I had no idea what could have brought such creature into our town let alone woods behind house… but something told me it wasn't just running off primal instinct anymore. Now felt more like unfinished business or some kind darkness finding its way out from under rock finally ready face world head…

All those nights spent watching horror movies had taught me one thing at least: once you find dead body should probably leave area pretty quick if want avoid becoming next victim yourself

But what choice did I really have?

If didn't go back tell them now then who would?

Back at the house, I phoned the cops in a calm steady voice, which was quite different from how I felt inside. Inside an hour they turned up. Having them there was like going from nowhere to somewhere. I showed them where it happened and did my best to explain what went down without saying anything about the hand that was too crazy for anyone to believe.

Obviously those guys were skeptical. A detached hand running around town is beyond belief. But they couldn't deny the evidence so they started searching the area instead. I hung back and thought terrible thoughts while the hand kept on getting bolder and doing worse things — now it had killed a kid. When that hit me, I almost passed out with horror.

While they were looking around, I went back to the mansion determined to find some way of ending it with this hand because she's/he's/they're not alone in this anymore if she ever was but we know that don't we once something gets you like that? So anyway now it wasn't just about saving myself but also about stopping more bad stuff from happening later on down the line somewhere else that might be closer than we think after all. All night long I pored over books and notes I'd taken from the library looking for any kind of clue that could help me figure out what needed done.

And then nightfall came, falling silently as death, or deeper if possible–the sort which descends when one is all alone in such situations as these; knowing full well help will never come though townsfolk may try their damnedest but damnedest won't be enough now or ever again either way.

Sitting there surrounded by flickering candlelight reading these old-ass books thinking god damnit why didn't he have any good stuff here steeled myself against what lay ahead determined no matter what even though only hours earlier hadn't yet reconciled myself yet (and who has?) to possibility that anything could be alive but when shadows started lengthening knew right away didn't i? Yeah. Somewhere out there in dark watching waiting ready to strike again. And fight had barely even begun.

Just before the police were ready to wrap up their initial search of the area, with no sign found of either child or any other traces whatsoever, the air grew heavy with suspicion. They must have thought I was involved somehow–or at least hiding something–and they weren't wrong. After all, what did I know about this? Nothing, except everything and more than anyone should ever have to know.

Deputy Reynolds was a big man – solid as a rock – and he made sure everyone knew it, including me. He lingered behind after sending the others off to start packing things up and motioned for me to join him near their cars.

“Mr. Loomis,” his voice boomed, “I’m gonna level with ya – this here situation is … what’s the word?” He looked around for a moment before coming back to me and continuing in an authoritative voice. “Unusual.”

I nodded slowly before returning his gaze steadily from beneath furrowed brows.

“We’re doin’ all we can,” he went on, “but if you’re not tellin’ us somethin’, now would be a real good time…”

His voice trailed off as he seemed to become aware of how futile his words were proving themselves against whatever force stood between us.

For my part, I stood there silent; squinting into the sun; rubbing my temples while thinking of everything that had happened so far; wondering what might come next

The last echoes of their departure were swallowed by the mansion in what seemed like oppressive silence. I was alone again, and it was then that I could feel the weight of the situation on my shoulders. It was a waking nightmare for me now, and a child had vanished – or worse – while I was unable to prevent further terrors from occurring.

Fear mixed with determination drove me back to the library. Those ancient books stared at me from their shelves, concealing their secrets behind enigmatic texts and cryptic symbols. Volume after volume I pulled down; book after book I spread across the table; anything that might describe how to destroy the hand or even contain its evil.

Hours passed as I read by candlelight, words blurring together until one passage caught my eye. It came from a treatise on demonology, bound in black leather with an uncomfortable crispness to each page. The passage detailed a ritual called "Binding of the Wandering Limb," employed during medieval times to restrain extremities animated by foul spirits. Rare herbs were required for this ritual along with a fresh sacrifice and a chant that must be recited beneath full moonlight.

It was far-fetched at best, veering into macabre and arcane territory, but it represented something tangible for once. Consulting the lunar calendar app on my phone told me there were three days until next full moon; this left little time for preparation and no margin of error whatsoever.

What needed doing next haunted my mind: materials for such rituals had to be gathered up first including those rare herbs which meant another trip into town would have to be made – this time over towards where an herbalist resides rather than venturing back through those woods we'd trekked earlier trying not think about things too hard concerning what exactly constitutes 'fresh' sacrifices nowadays besides perhaps some nice new blood given freely … but before that list could take shape in front of me there came pause as if my shaking hand had caught onto something. The enormity of what lay ahead filled every corner inside me, overwhelming through and through: never had I been one who dabbled in occultism nor believed in supernatural events so here it is that I find myself plotting out ancient forgotten rites against a disembodied hand which should not be.

Around me creaked mansion walls reminding that were not alone still – somewhere within or just beyond these very same wall parts there lurked watching waiting… Its motives remained unclear whilst its potentialities became frightfully apparent; therefore, time was running away too fast for my liking.

As the candle flickered and cast its long room shadows, I prepared myself mentally for what was to come over next few days. There was so much left and only limited hours remained before an encounter could happen which neither sidestep nor drag out any further. This meant going back into town once more but this occasion would see us head towards where an herbalist resides before stopping off at some point along way back home thinking about what constitutes fresh sacrifices nowadays besides nice new blood given freely…

I paused writing list of things required from me and trembled slightly while holding pen above paper surface; such realization overwhelmed entirety of being mine since never had believe or even think twice about such matters thus finding oneself deeply involved with ancient unknown rituals aimed at combating existence disembodied hands within haunted houses definitely did seem right thing do.

Mansion groaned around me, pressing on my awareness like an unspoken presence. Somewhere in these walls—or just outside them—was the hand, watching, waiting. What it wanted, I didn't know, but it was becoming increasingly clear how powerful it was. And with every second that passed, the more desperate I became to stop it.

The light from the candle flickered and danced across the room as I steeled myself for what lay ahead. Time was slipping away; there were things that needed to be done. The hand had thrown down the gauntlet, and I couldn't refuse. As the final flicker of the candle died, plunging me into darkness, I knew that the battle had only just begun – I was racing against unknown forces with no understanding of my own and stakes higher than ever before.

CHAPTER 5:

Dug Up Stories

It was a foggy morning. There was something about it that made everything seem dull and lifeless in Willow's End. I hadn't slept well, haunted by nightmares that left me shivering and gasping for breath long before the sun came up. The visions had been vivid; the hand, its fingers digging through dirt and skin alike, burrowing into graves and pulling out things that should have stayed buried.

Knowing that any delay could be fatal, I forced myself out of bed with limbs heavy from hours of restless tossing. Today, I needed to track down the supplies for the ritual outlined in the demonology tome. It felt absurd to think about performing what amounted to a medieval binding rite on a disembodied hand, but fear has a way of making nonsense necessary.

Breakfast was quickly taken standing, though not without its share of sidelong glances from my landlady. She'd seen me after every sleepless night this week; unsteady hands pouring milk over cereal as if they belonged to someone else entirely.

The streets were empty as I walked into town. The storm clouds still rolled low and brooding overhead — maybe people took it as an omen when children went missing — but also there was just something off in the air since Ashcroft's daughter vanished; some kind of unease humming underneath everyone's skin like electricity.

My first stop was the local herbalist: a creaky shop sandwiched between a boarded-up bakery and a dusty antiques store with half its inventory sitting outside under tarps because no one wanted anything to do with them anymore.

The bell above the door shrieked like metal against teeth when I stepped inside. The shop smelled dark; heavy with dried herbs and flowers so old they'd forgotten how to let go of their fragrance even after death.

Jars lined every wall from floor to ceiling, each filled with a different color or texture of plant parts, all tagged with handwritten labels that had faded and curled until the names were nearly illegible.

“Can I help you?” The voice came from the back of the shop; a raspy thing that scraped over my eardrums like gravel. A moment later, an elderly woman in an apron shuffled into view, her long grey hair wild around her face. Her eyes were sharp and assessing — wolf’s eyes.

“I need some very specific herbs for... a project I’m working on,” I started hesitantly, not sure how much to reveal.

She didn’t blink. “Tell me what hurts,” she said. “I’ve got everything from boneset to belladonna.”

I handed her the list from the book, my hand shaking so slightly I could pretend it wasn’t doing it at all. She took it without comment, scanning the contents with just a touch of speed-reading skill before she nodded slowly.

“You’re collecting quite the menagerie here,” she said finally, tone bordering on impressed as she squinted down at me through eyes that had seen too many years and carried too many secrets. “Some of these are powerful things, child. Old things. Not used much anymore.” She looked up again suddenly and smiled then — though there was nothing warm about it — like she’d won some kind of game against herself. “You dabbling in the dark arts?”

“Something like that,” I replied after a weighted pause, deciding honesty might be more useful than evasion this time around. “I’ve... run into a situation at Ashcroft’s.”

But instead of shock or fear, her face just lit up in understanding; like I'd come home to something we'd both known was waiting for me since the day we first met.

"I thought so when you walked through my door," she murmured under her breath almost tenderly, turning away from me to rummage through a set of shelves on the opposite wall. "That place..." she trailed off, but I knew what she meant.

When she handed me the herbs — each in their own protective little packet and jar — her touch was fleeting, like she didn't want to get too close to whatever had hitched a ride into town on my skin.

"Handle these with care," she warned instead of goodbye. "They're not for the faint of heart."

I tucked them gently into my bag next to the book as thanks died before it could reach my mouth and left without looking back.

She wasn't wrong about the air in there; when I stepped out onto the sidewalk again, it felt like waking up from anesthesia.

"In days of yore, much blood was used. A little will do — and it need not be human, thank God. I'd hope an ounce from some living thing should work."

I nodded with relief, knowing that I would have to interpret that final part carefully and responsibly.

When I left the apothecary's shop, something shifted inside me. The weight of what I had to do still pressed against my chest, but now that the first steps had been taken, it felt more like a burden I could bear. But the next thing on my list was going to be hard. To prepare for the ritual under the full moon, I had to find someplace secluded where the ground hadn't been touched by shadows of the past.

I decided to start in the area around the mansion. The land was rough; there were jagged upcroppings of stone and trees growing every which way but up — their limbs reaching skyward like arms trying to swim back up from underwater.

As I walked, I stumbled upon an old graveyard with its gates rusted and hanging open at odd angles. The tombstones were worn and covered in moss; you could barely read whose name lay etched beneath each one. It was a place forgotten by time but soaked with sadness nonetheless; a reminder of lives ended long ago and souls perhaps not at rest.

It sent a chill down my spine: This might just be exactly where to hold the ritual. It was isolated — out in history-haunted nowhere under wide-open sky — but also … in a graveyard? That seemed wrong somehow; disrespectful even. My conscience wrestled with itself because either way you looked at it there was no getting around doing something very bad or letting something very bad go on being done.

So what I decided to do instead was this: Move out onto sacred ground while still keeping within reach of its energy — set up just beyond its walls.

By the time dusk fell and the moon began to rise, casting its silver glow over everything, I had gathered all my herbs; lit all the candles; created all the ambiance for a night that would decide my fate — and maybe Willow's End. The wind started to blow harder at this point, running through the trees like it had voices in it from far back whispering something cautionary or guiding as I began my chant to hold or let loose the darkness at Ashcroft's core.

CHAPTER 6:

Blood On The Glass

The ritual left me physically exhausted and mentally vulnerable. Strange things started to happen after the bloodbath. The whole cemetery was illuminated by a cold white light coming from the full moon, which made even the longest shadows dance and shake like living beings. When I finished chanting, a silence so deep it seemed as though it were holding its breath came over everything.

It felt like entering another world when I went back into the house. What had previously been an atmosphere of oppressive stillness now crackled with awareness; it was as if the walls themselves were conscious of what I had done on their doorstep. Every creak and groan of the old building seemed louder than ever before, rattling my already frayed nerves.

But this was nothing compared to what awaited me in the library where I'd last seen it…the hand. The glass case that housed it was shattered, shards winking maliciously up from under patches of moonlight that streamed through gaps in heavy curtains onto polished boards…which were also smeared with fresh red trails.

My heart thudded sickeningly against ribs as I moved closer, musty air mingling with metallic tang from newly spilled blood. Following these droplets – scattered across floor and splashed up wall like something dragged itself or wriggled along- led straight out through corridor toward main hall.

Every step vibrated house, each settling groan more insistent than before - 'more alive' should have said - but unhappy about my presence.

Trail stopped at bottom step grand staircase; here lay one policeman whose body language told story clearly enough: terror etched into uplifted eyes set wide apart staring blankly ahead while mouth hung open mid-scream forever silenced by severed windpipe…or something equally grotesque…

But I had to notify the others first—the police detail outside, the citizens. Trembling, my phone was in my hand and I dialed emergency services. The voice that came out of me when I reported what I saw was barely recognizable as my own.

After my call, I armed myself with the heaviest bookend from the library—a single piece of carved marble—and went deeper into the mansion. Darkness pressed down on me; it was filled with dying and dead sounds and every shadow seemed like it could be a threat flinching.

It felt like the house itself was moving against me. Doors that had been open were closed for no reason, while others that had been closed creaked wide as soon as they heard me near them; some unseen force seemed to guide them. The air was cold, too cold, and every breath felt like inhaling ice.

I kept going because there was nothing else I could do. Each step took me further into the heart of darkness that used to be called Ashcroft Mansion in better days; each step brought another horror closer to being face-to-face with me. So when a soft sound like something crawling skittered around a corner up ahead, I didn't run. This time it's close – this time I can feel it – and so this time: let it come for me.

CHAPTER 7:
First Night

The night wrapped around the house and made it groan and creak. It was a haunted symphony, an eerie noise that crept through the passages as if it were secrets spoken in hushed voices. The rain had come back, hammering down on the roof with a drumming, repetitive force that only heightened what was already there. I couldn't sleep; every shadow felt like it could hide danger in its folds, and every sound seemed pregnant with menace after the hand.

But my eyes were heavy from exhaustion, weighted down by fear until they were too sharp to bear. So I just propped up a dresser against the bedroom door and called it good enough. My muscles shook afterward but it was that or fight-or-flight forever.

The room was cold and full of drafts — the brittle heating system did nothing to block them out through cracked windows, so I wound myself up in a threadbare blanket found at the foot of the bed instead. It smelled musty but that bothered me less than freezing to death.

I watched shadows flicker in corners cast by candlelight I'd set on the nightstand — they looked like grotesque shapes dancing on wallpaper; twisted things writhing where they shouldn't be alive. After watching a hand flop around where it shouldn't have been able to, anything could look like fingers or palms now.

The storm outside picked up again; wind howled like regretting wraiths who never got to unburden themselves about all those unknown sorrows they'd borne witness to over their lonely lives. One blow was louder than usual — something banged downstairs sharply enough that it startled even me out of my brooding vigil. Heart leaping into throat, I waited for another. Wasn't sure if I wanted one or not.

Minutes stretched longer than this house itself is old while I sat there frozen solid still trying to hear over the storm. There it was again — a scrape on the floorboards below, softer but more distinct than before. Something dragging; something solid but unsure. Couldn't be, I thought, but already knew — it was moving.

So fear took one hand and knowledge the other and made me move my feet across the cold boards until I was standing beside the bed with candle in hand. The floor was freezing on my feet when I crept over to the door, and every instinct told me not to open it, but they also told me that this — whatever all this is — is something you can't back away from or run from or hide from.

I pushed dressers inches at a time until there was just enough space for a person to slip through the crack of an open door into a dimly lit hallway with no end in sight. My shadow stretched distorted across the floor behind me like a sentinel in these halls of hell.

The hallway was empty when I looked outside, all doors tight shut; but still, beneath pitter-pattered silence upstairs there came soft continuous scrapes down hardwood steps that chilled with their persistence. So I gathered up what I had left and went out toward them.

The library door swung mostly closed then swayed back open softly as if playing coy without its partner. Inside it was dark except for when lightning licked shelves taller than anything here should be and stroked covers wider than any could contain. But after one flash there came only quiet so heavy you could feel it humming in your bones like waiting does.

My heart raced as I approached with only the dim light of my candle to guide me through the oppressive blackness. Somewhere deeper in the library, my foot brushed against something soft and yielding on the floor. I jumped back in horror and pointed the candle downward, stifling a scream.

It was a rat. Or what used to be a rat. The thing had been torn apart; its insides were spread out over the polished wood like someone's idea of a sick joke. It wasn't even cold yet; blood still shone wetly in the candlelight.

The hand had not just been searching—it was hunting, feeding maybe. And this was its lair, perhaps with me among next victims.

Just then the air moved like it does when there's no wind, and the candle sputtered wildly, casting odd shadows around the room. I turned slowly, dread hardening into frozen terror inside me as my eyes found what had caused that draft.

Across from me, high up on one of the shelves at far end of room, sat severed hand. Alive. It tapped fingers against leather-bound spine of some very old book—tapped in time with rhythm nobody could hear but both of us. Then it stopped tapping and looked at me.

I don't mean it turned head or bent wrist to get better look—whole damn thing looked at me: eyes met mine (mine alive with horror; its empty but somehow still accusing). In that instant between one heartbeat and next I discovered that there is more than one way for hunter to find itself hunted.

For another few seconds we stood there like that: me stuck fast where I was by overwhelming fear; it balanced on books across room from where I cowered near door, watching without eyes but seeing nonetheless (its gaze burning into mine till thought could take root).

Then hand's fingers started twitching again—twisting this way then that—as if trying to tell me something or just mocking my terror with silhouette no sane mind could understand. My own raced trying to make sense of it all—how can such thing be real, let alone show so much wicked smart?

After it had considered me while longer, hand began to move. But not like you'd expect: no clumsy shuffle across floor; instead fingers acted as legs might for some kind spider and it crawled—yes CRAWLED!—down from where sat on topmost shelf full of ancient dusty tomes bound in animal skin. It was quiet too, no sound save for softest whispering.

I took step back then holding candle moved shakey-held breath quick-spaced gasping pain through close around squeeze heart my although feet-frozen should've run away long before this point walls that were surely figures morphing arm lengths cast towering bookshelves shadows staring down horror continuing towards trapped realization hit mind raced edge large table wood spine solid cold behind beyond nothingness filled fear into unrelenting steady pace hand creeping-the-.

With a blast of adrenaline, I pushed the table by the candle and threw down some heavy books. They smashed to the ground with loud thumps, momentarily numbing the hand. So, I grabbed at something within reach – an ancient tome bound in thick leather that listed maritime laws – and chucked it with all my might at its arm.

The book landed perfectly, trapping the hand beneath itself against the floor. Its fingers wriggled and twitched wildly back and forth while scrabbling uselessly at the polished wood. It was a sickening but fascinating sight; a human intellect warring with an alien malevolence in order to survive.

Not stopping to watch, I spun around on my heel and raced out into the hallway, bursting through its doors as if they were paper. The mansion had ceased being merely sinister or enigmatic; now it was a battleground where I lacked any chance of victory.

I slammed shut the door behind me once outside of the library and leaned back against it while gasping for air. The silence which followed seemed almost as fearful as what had come before – every creak or whisper from inside could have been announcing some new terror about to befall me. But for now, at least – I was safe.

I knew this wouldn't last long though; books alone wouldn't hold back that hand forever. What I needed was a more permanent solution: some method by which either destruction or containment could be achieved before any further harm came to people (or things).

My brain raced as I hurried along corridors towards where local knowledge indicated there ought be stored such information: dusty old chests filled with forgotten volumes detailing rituals performed years past; legends passed down through generations spoken only around firesides on moonless nights when whiskey flowed like water whereupon spirits rose higher still.

Pressing forward toward study where additional texts related specifically to area history combined with folklore would likely reside given previous observations made while seeking answers regarding said nightmare; awareness heightened by awareness that appeared insignificant at time but has since assumed grave importance.

CHAPTER 8:

The Start Of The Chase

The darkness in the mansion grew as I went into the study; it was like a foggy cloud of doom. Every corner had an eye with invisible powers, and every crack in the wooden floor might have been produced by that abominable hand creeping up behind you. But fear gave me strength; it made me more determined than ever to find some way of stopping this terrible thing.

The moment I stepped into the study, I saw row upon row of old books. The spines were broken and faded from years of disuse. The smell of yellowing paper filled my nostrils — now tinged with danger after everything that had happened. I started rifling through them all, looking for something — anything — about local legends or occult practices that might point me toward a clue to defeating whatever supernatural force I was up against.

It was while I sifted through these dusty old things that I heard it: a faint scraping sound, so slight it might almost have been imagined. My heart stopped. Slowly, carefully turning around, I half expected to see that hand come skittering toward me across the floor. But there was nothing: The room lay quiet as a tomb (except for the flickering candlelight casting its eerie shadows on every wall).

Thinking maybe my nerves were getting the best of me, I turned back around — only to be met with a sudden cold breeze brushing against my neck. All the windows were closed; there shouldn't have been any draft at all. My eyes shot out in search of where this fresh chill could have come from just in time to see...a book slightly out of place on one shelf...its cover cracked open as if someone had recently leafed through it.

Moving slowly toward it, step by cautious step, I realized it wasn't actually a book at all but some kind of cleverly disguised lever. Taking a deep breath, I pulled it — and watched in amazement as a hidden panel of the wall swung open to reveal a narrow, dark passageway. The air that whooshed out was cool and damp, smelling of earth and decay.

Driven by equal parts fear and curiosity, I snatched up my lantern and stepped inside. Stone lined the walls; dust coated the floor thickly enough that no one had set foot on this path in centuries. The deeper into this secret tunnel I went, the more it seemed like the oppressive darkness was swallowing up my light source, making the way ahead stretch on forever.

Finally, after what felt like hours of walking but was probably no more than a few minutes' time, the passage emptied into a small underground chamber. My nose was met with the unmistakable smell of mildew — along with something else: something sickly sweet yet rotten that instantly turned my stomach. That's when I saw it: In the center of this room stood an altar, large enough for two grown men to lay side by side upon if they wished. It was made of stone, blackened by age and use alike; but it wasn't just age that had stained this particular rock's surface — there were fresh stains too, still wet-looking in certain spots (and glistening under my lantern light). Stains which could only be one thing...blood.

On the altar were the leftovers of what seemed to be different small animals, each of them cut open and arranged in a gory act of ritualistic slaughter. The scene was horrendous, with bodies ripped apart neatly along predetermined lines and their innards spread out like some macabre form of art. It was definitely done by the hand; its wicked signature was all over this mess.

My head spun at the ferocity displayed here, and I felt sick as I got closer to this sacrificial table. But as my eyes scanned across the blood-stained arrangement before me, it occurred to me that every animal had been placed according to its position within a circle inscribed with a pentagram. Following the lines that formed this star inside another shape which looked like five triangles put together too closely for comfort, I noticed that there sat unlit black candles on every one of them.

The realization that what we had here wasn't just mindless violence hit me like a bucket full of ice water; it was part of something much larger than itself — an ancient forbidden rite perhaps? performed by none other than our own hands? For fear whereof should such dire consequences arise, they also know how best can these half-rotted brains wrap around knowledge concerning such matters?

I turned away from it quickly so not even thinking about looking back again until later when will have time but instead took out my camera phone hoping someone smarter than me might be able to figure out what any or all these symbols mean if anything at all besides being random scribbles made up on spot during last night's vodka-fueled binge watched too much Netflix series about witchcraft then went online read Wikipedia article titled "Paganism 101 for Beginners." After snapping few more pics just case anyone asks whether seen sorry haven't got slightest CLUE! So packed up stuff threw over shoulder headed downstairs so fast ran straight into wall didn't even see coming before tripped over cat no idea we even owned but somehow made it down into kitchen where grabbed bottle wine poured glass sat there sipping while watching sun rise thinking about everything that just happened wondering whether should call police or what exactly? You know what forget it can't deal with this right now gonna go take bath maybe wash off some this craziness.

Getting the necessary stuff around the house, I get ready to go back beneath it. The idea of returning to that gruesome sight terrified me, but doing nothing was infinitely more dangerous. I armed myself with a large iron crowbar both for the ritual and protection in case the hand tried to intervene.

As I walked through the hidden passage again, the air felt colder, the darkness thicker. Each step was heavy as if I were descending into earth's very core. When I reached the chamber, my stomach churned once at the sight of blood stained altar but I steeled myself and began setting up counter-ritual.

I drew protective symbols at strategic points around altar and muttered ancient incantations while sprinkling salt in wide circle. Words were unfamiliar on my tongue – language forgotten by time; and with each word uttered – even though silently vibrating through air seemed impossible because stillness cloaked everything underground.

When everything had been set up, I took few steps back holding tightly onto iron crowbar then spoke final words of incantation. A wind started blowing from nowhere which seemed to be coming all directions simultaneously thus causing candle flames burn almost horizontally due its strength before dying down completely leaving behind eerie silence where malevolence hung so thickly one could almost touch it.

Just as suddenly as it had started blowing, wind ceased; heavy quietness fell upon room like blanket. Foulness withdrew itself from atmosphere till only emptiness remained -as though something got sucked out from space itself.

For what felt like eternity but was actually just few minutes during which time seemed irrelevant while heart pounded against chest wall gasping for breaths half-expecting sightless thing crawl across floor towards me however there came no sign nor sound indicative presence either movement made approach toward Evil lurking somewhere unseen so cautiously took some paces closer peering into gloom cast shadows about altar wherefore maleficent limb might hide yet found nothing: apparently, spell had worked; hand had been banished.

Relief washed over me like tidal wave mingling with exhaustion; I had stopped the rite. However, this could only be short-term success because somewhere out there was still that hand – its motives unknown but surely wicked. Therefore, I should find it destroy completely before another rite is attempted or more damage caused.

I left chamber sealing entrance behind me feeling resolve harden within. The hunt was not finished; it had hardly started. No longer just fearful place full of secrets and terrors, mansion became battleground where nightmares cease forever.

CHAPTER 9:
Friends And Foes

After the ritual's intensity and a difficult night, the mansion appeared to be at peace. My body felt hollow, but my mind surged with what I had to do next — the hand was still out there somewhere, and it hadn't lost any of its power when we interrupted its ceremony. But in Willow's End, trust was hard to come by.

So I decided I would give the town another visit in the morning under the pretense of gathering more supplies. The early light cast long shadows on the quaint streets, and as I walked through them it seemed like the chill from the house stuck close behind me — like a wet cloth.

At the diner, people were talking quietly with each other in ways that suggested superstition mingled with fear. Conversation after conversation centered around recent disturbances at and around

Ashcroft Mansion — words weighed heavy with dread and macabre curiosity. I nursed a lukewarm coffee when Reverend Thomas slid into the booth across from me. The town's elderly pastor wore kind eyes that held more understanding than most.

"Mr. Loomis, isn't it?" he asked in a soft voice that betrayed an intensity beneath his gaze — as if something deep sat behind those eyes that knew much more than they should.

"That's right," I replied, cautious but game for playing along.

"I heard you've taken up residence at Ashcroft place," he continued after folding his hands atop of table. "That property been harboring dark rumors for as long as I remember. Most folks 'round here stay clear."

"Yeah," I said testing waters with semi-honesty. "The mansion seems to have some… history."

"More 'n history," he lowered his voice even further. "Legacy o' darkness — some say cursed itself; there've been incidents over years — disappearances; strange sightings, too… You seen enough already out there to know there's more 'n a little truth in them tales."

I paused, then nodded. Trust has to start somewhere and Reverend Thomas' straightforward demeanor made me feel like taking a chance. "There is something in that house," I admitted quietly — "something not right. I've encountered it."

The Reverend’s eyes grew dark and serious. "I feared as much. This ain’t just about ghosts or simple hauntings, Mr. Loomis… There are older, deeper magics at work here — have you ever heard of the Binding of Silas Ashcroft?"

"No," I confessed, suddenly intrigued.

"Silas Ashcroft dabbled in necromancy; he was tryin' to keep himself alive by any means necessary... When the town found out what he was doing they performed a ritual to bind his spirit and keep it from doin' further harm, but now it seems like maybe that binding didn’t stick so good…"

"That would explain some things," I said thinking back on all those horrible visions.

Reverend Thomas nodded gravely. "I can help you — maybe show you how to strengthen the binding or reseal it — but we gotta be careful: dark spirits don't take kindly to being thwarted, an’ they usually protect themselves with violence."

Thankful for the offer and too aware of my need for every possible aid, I agreed to meet him at church later that day so we could talk more about what our plan might look like. Leaving diner gave me a flicker of hope, though — even if it was small when compared against everything else before us.

After coming back to the mansion, I did not have much time before Reverend Thomas might suggest a ritual, so I went into town and bought some things from the small market there — salt, iron nails and more candles. But no matter how ordinary these errands were, they could not distract me from my growing fear of returning to the house.

The mansion seemed angrier than ever when I came back. Doors slammed shut as I passed them; whispers echoed down the hallways, just out of understanding. I was being watched — stalked by something that did not want its secrets found out.

That night, before meeting with Reverend Thomas, I decided to check on the room where I had first encountered the hand. The door creaked ominously as I pushed it open; beyond lay a room bathed in the fading light of a sun setting behind dirty windows.

What met my eyes was grotesque — a scene of death. Rats, birds and what looked like small feral animals from the woods nearby were laid out in a sickening imitation of the ritual I had disrupted: their bodies arranged in a precise pattern; each carcass expertly flayed open with their insides exposed and arranged in some chillingly artistic fashion.

The message was clear: not only was the hand loose but it also seemed to be stepping up its macabre activities — perhaps gathering power or simply thumbing its nose at my attempts to stop it. The coppery smell of blood filled my nostrils, and bile rose in my throat. But this had to end — soon. Clenching my jaw, I documented what I saw with my camera; each flash seemed to summon another curse on that place or bring about another doomed soul.

I stepped quickly away from that hellhole and shut the door behind me with a shudder. The images burned into my brain acted as an instant reminder of what we were fighting against. The hand was not just some passive thing; it was alive — actively malevolent, growing stronger and bolder with each act.

As the last light of day vanished from the sky, I went to meet Reverend Thomas in the church. The building could not have been more different from the mansion — peaceful, with candles flickering softly against stained glass windows, casting colored patterns on a stone floor. The Reverend was waiting for me at the altar, an open book in front of him.

"Mr Loomis," he greeted me solemnly. "I've made some notes on the original binding ritual. It seems we may have to do parts of it again."

He motioned for me to join him, and together we pored over the ancient text: written in Latin mixed with local dialect; instructions interspersed with warnings and notes on necessary precautions. This would not be easy. Specific astrological conditions were required (thankfully nearly upon us) as well as materials already gathered — but most disturbingly also demanded a personal sacrifice; physical and spiritual offering of blood.

"Binding won't hold unless anchored in physical realm," Reverend Thomas said gravely. "That means blood Mr. Loomis – are you prepared for that?"

I nodded heavily. "Yes; whatever it takes."

"Good," he said, shutting the book loudly. "Time is short. It must be done tonight at midnight, when the thinness of the veil between worlds is greatest."

Spending those hours in preparation, we collected several holy relics from the church—objects that had been blessed and sanctified—while I made one last trip to the mansion for some additional items I had gathered during my encounters with the supernatural. Each step felt like moving deeper into a dark tunnel, though I could see a light at its end: my confrontation with the hand.

When it grew close to midnight, we returned to the silent mansion, our footsteps echoing through empty hallways and on old wooden floors. The Reverend told me to set up our ritual space in the main hall—the epicenter of paranormal activity—and so we drew ancient symbols on the floor together, arranged candles in a precise configuration around them and set out our offerings.

At midnight we began. The Reverend chanted in Latin (his voice became distant as it echoed through other parts of the halls), and I followed suit as best I could below him. It grew colder around us; flames flickered on still air as if blown by wind through windows too far away to open.

Then all was broken by another sound from upstairs—a crash like breaking glass—and after pausing for a moment to listen we continued with greater haste. Seconds later there came a low dragging noise down the staircase that grew louder every second it went on.

And then it appeared at top—the severed hand dragging itself along banister toward bottom—but stopped when it reached bottom as if surveying scene before it. Its skin was pale and almost seemed to glow in candlelight; moved with purpose that was terrible only because whatever drove this thing lacked any sense or humanity whatsoever.

Father Thomas' chants grew more intense as his voice rose above sound of hand's approach; iron rod ready in hand—I stood over circle. The hand seemed to hesitate then charged forward across floor toward it.

Just as it crossed the threshold of our drawn symbols, there was a flash like lightning and a crash like thunder through hall. The hand stopped inches from us, its fingers twitching spasmodically for a moment before going still—finally quelled by power of ritual.

Reverend Thomas and I stood there breathing heavily, looking at each other with relief mixed equally with exhaustion on our faces. The ritual had worked—the hand was bound again. But as we stood there, surrounded by still-twitching relic in flickering candlelight, we knew this wasn't over. Not even close. The darkness at Ashcroft Mansion ran deep and wide, and more awaited us within its walls. But for now we had secured an important victory; even though night remained blacker than ever before, it also seemed mere degrees less threatening—at least temporarily.

CHAPTER 10:

Midnight In The Mansion

The stillness that came after the ritual did not last long. Even as Reverend Thomas and I were putting away the materials we'd used, there was a draught through the hall which should have been impossible with all the windows and doors closed. It seemed like the house itself was sighing—a deep, slow exhale of relief or perhaps anger. We looked at each other, knowing that what had happened was just one fight won out of many yet to come.

I walked him to the door and thanked him for his help and courage. "Be careful, Mr. Loomis," he said gravely. "This place... it's a dark energy intersection. You've bound one evil here tonight but there may be others lurking in these shadows."

I heard his words echo in my head as I locked up again, feeling alone once more. The mansion groaned louder than ever in the aftermath, like it knew something had gone down tonight. Too tired to sleep, too wired to rest, I decided to go on patrol through the house; who knows what might still be hiding?

My flashlight cut through the darkness as I moved from room to room along corridors buried in shadow. I don't think anyone who hasn't done it knows how much noise their own footsteps can make when they're creeping around an empty house where everything echoes. I kept staring at my heart pounding out of my chest.

When I got to the library—where things always seemed to happen—I swept my light across shelf after shelf of books muttering secrets under their breath. Then I heard it. Softly a moan. My breath caught as I swung around looking for whatever made that sound. The moan came again. This time longer. Louder and more anguished. I followed it back behind one of the shelves.

With fear weighing me down, I got closer. The moaning grew louder. More desperate. I touched it—the bookshelf—and it swung silently open. There was another passage behind it, one I hadn't known about. My heart skipped a beat as I realized there might be layers to this house I'd never seen.

It was narrow and choked with cobwebs. The air smelled like it hadn't been used in years. I should have turned back; I knew that. But how could I? Not when someone—or something—was moaning like that. I had to follow the sound. It spoke of pain. And if there was some suffering soul somewhere in here, how could I turn away?

The hallway twisted and turned so much that you would've thought whoever designed it didn't want anyone finding their way through. Finally it opened up into a small dimly lit room. And what I saw there was worse than anything my imagination had come up with.

Chains hung from the walls. In the middle of the room, a person was shackled. Their body was emaciated. Their skin pale and covered in wounds. It was a man. His eyes were wide open but looked empty. He seemed alive but barely: his lips cracked, as he whispered hoarsely for us to let him go.

"Help me," he rasped. "Please. Release me from this."

I rushed over to him, checking the locks on the chains. They were ancient and rusty, and I didn't have a key. With nothing left to lose, I took the iron bar that was still in my hand. A couple of powerful swings later, and the chains broke off.

He fell into my arms like a ragdoll; with all the strength drained out of him, he couldn't stand up straight anymore.

"Who did this?" I asked as I helped him sit against the wall.

"The hand... it brought me here," he said in a hoarse whisper. "Forced me to... serve it... perform rituals..."

Fear crawled through me when I understood what he was saying. The hand hadn't only been an agent of chaos—it had enslaved this man for its own nefarious purposes. His condition showed just how much power and malevolence that thing possessed.

"Rest now," I said, draping my coat over him. "You're safe."

But as soon as I finished speaking, a cold laughter rattled down the hallway: mirthless, empty, chilling to the bone. Dread poured through me like ice water — we weren't done yet. We were still deep within these walls' clutches; we had only bound the hand of darkness that lurked here.

I got him back on his feet again and half-carried his weakened body through the passage. It felt like the mansion was watching us now; where its silence had been calm before, now it was hostile. When we came back into the corridor and started heading toward where we'd completed the ritual—the relief of success seemed years away in comparison with what waited for us in those shadows.

We needed to leave—get outside its reach before this place could take us again — but when we got there something stopped me dead: realization struck like lightning —the mansion wasn't going let us walk out scot-free. The front doors were locked tight; they wouldn't budge an inch.

I looked back at him, saw the same terror in his eyes that was gripping my own chest. “We have find another way out,” I said, feeling a hard knot of determination settle in my gut. The night was still young, and we had only just begun to fight for our lives.

CHAPTER 11:

Message In Blood

This house seemed narrower, more oppressive as if the air itself was thickening against us. The man we saved clung heavily to my arm, his breath shallow and ragged. We moved slowly, each step echoing ominously in the silence that once again fell over the building.

I needed to find another way out — a back door, perhaps, or a service entrance not sealed by the malevolent will of this place. But the weight of his arm across my shoulders kept me focused on one thing: time was running out.

He stopped suddenly, squeezing my arm so hard I winced. “It’s here,” he whispered hoarsely, his eyes wide with fear.

Confused, I followed his gaze down the hallway. At first I saw only darkness — shadows cast by some distant flickering light — but then my eyes adjusted to it and I could see that there was a red glow coming from around the corner. I hesitated for a moment, unsure what fresh hell awaited us there but knowing we had no choice but to face it.

When we turned that corner, though...I froze. The walls were covered in fresh-looking blood that dripped slowly down into grotesque patterns which seemed to pulse slightly in the dim light. And at about eye level with me there was a message written in huge characters traced out by some substance too thick and slow-moving to be anything other than blood: "RETURN WHAT IS MINE."

The sight was so jarringly overt that for a moment I couldn't even process its subtler implications—the fact that whatever hand (or intelligence behind it) had written these words wasn't just moving objects around anymore; it was communicating directly with us now. Demanding something back—presumably referring either to those binding-ritual items or else seeking reunification with its own other parts through them.

"I...I can't go any further," the man murmured, collapsing against the wall. His face was ashen, his eyes haunted by what he'd seen and what it meant.

I helped him sit down, my mind racing. I couldn't leave him alone—but I needed to continue exploring. "Stay here," I said, trying to keep my voice steadier than I felt. "I'll look ahead for an exit and come back immediately."

He nodded weakly, gripping my hand for a moment with surprising strength. "Watch yourself," he exhaled – a plea freighted with the weight of knowing only too well what dangers waited in these shadows.

Leaving him in the relative safety of the hallway, I moved forward into the deeper redness of that glow's source. As I neared its end-of-hallway location, the air grew colder and heavier around me—more oppressive—as though now I walked into the very heart of this house's darkness.

The source turned out to be a small study off one side of this hall; its door was partially ajar when I reached it. But when I pushed it open...god. The whole room must have been painted crimson: blood everywhere on every surface; furniture upturned or smashed outright; old stains mingling messily with fresh wetnesses on walls and ceiling alike... And at center stage amidst all this doom-strewn décor sat another collection like those animals' corpses from before—not just rats now but birds too (sparrows mostly), plus larger rodents (moles?), even some kind of marmot-looking thing whose head had been twisted completely 'round so its face looked up at us inside-out through empty eye sockets still leaking tears which mixed subtly there with droplets from our own terrified gazes back down upon them—

each creature arranged more elaborately than any previous example had been, each seemingly having met its violent end only minutes earlier at most

Knowing that the hand was gaining ground made my skin crawl. It was establishing a stronghold, a source of power from which it could operate. And it would not be satisfied until everything it thought had been taken away from it is returned.

In anticipation of disgust and fear overwhelming me, I tiptoed carefully around the grisly decorations, looking for any other way out of the room. There, behind a moth-eaten curtain, I saw a small window. It was old and painted shut but I had to try something. I used an iron rod to pry at the edges and after much creaking and groaning from the wood, it finally gave.

A rush of fresh air swept into the stuffy room like a tiny balm against its oppressive claustrophobia. Moving as fast as possible without making too much noise or drawing attention to myself in any other way, I wiggled open space enough for one person to squeeze through.

Back in the hallway again, I helped him up off his knees and guided him back towards where we'd found him earlier – near what now served as our makeshift living quarters during this nightmare scenario: The study room adjacent to where we'd first entered into this maze-like mansion's labyrinthine interiority hours ago… "We can get out this way," I explained.

With considerable effort on both our parts (him being weakened by whatever forces were keeping him captive here), we managed to get his body through the window first; he fell forward onto soft earth outside with an audible sigh before collapsing completely thereupon… Then came my turn: Pulling myself up onto windowsill ledges while simultaneously pushing/lifting oneself downward/forward/outward through tight spaces between walls made much more difficult due not only aforementioned weakness but also own apparent size/strength relative difference betwixt us two humans involved herein as well…

Upon emerging from within these confines, one finds oneself facing outward toward/against outer surfaces comprising rest of world outside building's boundaries proper. In this instance, there stood before us only one such structure: A sprawling Victorian manor whose silhouette loomed ominously against darkened sky above; its countless windows seemed like eyes peering down at us even now – though we lay prone upon ground below them instead. Night still cloaked everything with deepest shade imaginable save when moonlight broke through cloud cover overhead but even then air felt lighter somehow than it had done indoors where malevolence had held sway until moments ago.

"We've got to get away from here," I told him, pulling him to his feet and keeping my eyes fixed on the mansion behind us. "As far as possible."

Together we stumbled away from that forbidding edifice while the night pressed ever closer around our backs as if to say: Not yet satisfied with mere respite are you? The true battle against this place will only just have begun once we're out of range, mark my words…

CHAPTER 12:

Rituals And Revelations

The night was deep and dark as we rushed from the mansion, the soil beneath our feet cold and unrelenting. Every step away from that damned place felt like a small victory but the chill in my bones told me that it might not be over -— and it wasn't.

We reached the town hours before dawn; its streets empty and silent. Michael —a man whose name I learned only recently— was in no condition to continue on without rest. We found solace in a small park on the outskirts of town, concealed behind a few trees. There, we collapsed onto a bench, our breath clouding in front of us.

In between shivers and gasps for air, Michael's story came out in bits and pieces. He had been a handyman for the town —known for his skill and his quiet nature— but his luck took a turn when he got too close to the mansion one night on a dare from friends who didn't believe in local legends. That was when the hand took him; using him for its rituals to strengthen its hold on this world.

"It used me to gather things… items of power," Michael told us through weak breaths filled with fear. "Books, artifacts—anything with energy. And then… then it can make you see things, horrible things." He paused here, swallowing hard before adding "Your mind isn't your own anymore."

His words sent shivers down my spine; this wasn't just some disembodied relic – it was an entity with immeasurable power over minds; bending wills at whim. I realized then that escaping from that house hadn't been liberation—it had been concession. Someone once said "the greatest trick devil ever pulled was convincing world he didn't exist" well I think escape may have just given us time enough to forget how many enemies there are waiting inside those walls.

As dawn broke over the horizon and painted the sky with pinks and golds, Michael's health deteriorated. He started speaking in broken sentences; delirious from fever.

"I have to get you medical attention," I said, helping him to his feet. His body felt like it could crumple under me at any moment.

He nodded weakly, but struggled to stand even with my support. We made our way slowly towards nearest hospital as morning grew brighter on sleepy town. The streets were filling up now; curious eyes glancing over at us but I kept moving forward until finally reaching entrance where we were met by wide eyed nurses who rushed him inside without question of what happened or why he looked so bad. I took this opportunity sit alone in waiting area for moment while doctors tended their patient —and found myself overwhelmed by events too fresh for reflection.

Fatigue crashed into me like a tidal wave: clothes stained and torn from nights rough trek through forested land, blood still oozing from cuts all over body but it was scars hidden deep within mind that hurt most.

While I sat there, sifting through our next steps, an elderly lady came up to me. From across the room she had been observing me, her eyes keen and perceptive.

"You've been to the old house, haven't you?" she murmured in a low voice.

I looked up, taken aback. "Yes. How did you know?"

She took a seat beside me with rigid posture and grave expression. "I was born in this town. I've seen what that place does to people. You seem like you've seen a ghost or something worse."

Her bluntness caused me to reveal more than I had intended; my words tumbled out like a confession. She listened closely, nodding as if my story confirmed her worst suspicions.

“That place is cursed—truly cursed,” she declared when I finished speaking. “But what you’re describing…it’s more than just hauntings; it’s an infestation, a blight of the darkest sort. You’ll need something stronger than prayers for that.”

Having made up her mind, she got to her feet again. “Come on. I know some people that we need to talk to others who have survived the mansion but fought back their way.”

Curious now and willing for any kind of assistance, I went after her. Allies were a slender hope, but hope nonetheless. As we left the hospital, the town seemed different: shadowed, uncertain yet filled with potential allies against Ashcroft Mansion’s darkness soon enough.

CHAPTER 13:

Ancestor's Curse

Mrs. Whitmore, an old woman, was the one who accompanied me. She led me through the winding streets of Willow's End until we reached a small house at the edge of town. But even if it was just humble and tucked away by huge gnarled trees that seemed to hide it from all wickedness in the world around it, there still hung about that dwelling in some way a feeling of quietness as though it were holding itself back from contact with anything dark or evil. This is where she told me I could find some answers and maybe allies against whatever malignant thing had taken up residence in this mansion.

The moment I stepped inside, books lined shelves while artifacts mingled with oddities across continents and ages—a collection as random as our enemy. Mrs. Whitmore introduced some people who had encountered supernatural forces personally; they had formed themselves into an organization called The Guardians whose objective was to monitor and neutralize any malevolent activities originating from Ashcroft Manor or its environs.

Edgar – a man with keen eyes but gentle manners—was the first to take charge in telling us what they knew about their mission there: “We’ve lost things at that place,” he started speaking slowly like his words carried weight behind them; then he sighed heavily before continuing more quietly than before “Lost friends… family members… peace… But we gained knowledge too; insights into how arcane arts work thanks to Silas Ashcroft.”

Sitting down among those people (each one having seen something strange), my hands trembled slightly when Mrs. Whitmore gave me a tea cup. Edgar kept talking: “Silas wasn’t just another landowner or hermit living outside town limits – He practiced black magic aimed towards obtaining immortality which failed horribly because his neighbors found out what he had done.”

Clara took over speaking next after listening patiently so far—her ageless face contradicted by sharp intelligent eyes which never blinked once while she narrated events from that point onwards; “The villagers didn’t understand… Silas had already set things into motion long before they could try chaining him up inside with locks or filling rooms apart from each other using holy water. He connected his spirit to the house, tying it down with his own severed hand.”

They went on and I sat there in a kind of horrified fascination as they explained how the mansion acted as a focal point for supernatural forces because of what Ashcroft did with necromancy – calling out beyond our world boundaries bringing spirits through. But it wasn't just haunted; it became cursed itself by becoming a beacon which attracted like-minded souls.

Interrupting himself briefly so I'd know we're still on same page, Edgar said "The hand you found is nothing more than an object manipulated by Siles's consciousness spread across this land like an infection. He may be dead but he still orchestrates these horrors from somewhere hidden within shadows."

It felt like being suffocated all at once; no longer were my nightmares mere products created accidentally by some lost ghostly individual's sad memories or bad experiences that wouldn't let them go – now they became calculated acts designed purposefully by ancient sorcerer who refused dying. Everything was bigger than before: not just another haunting but rather full-blown war against eternal desire.

I asked feeling helpless, "How do we fight something that's already dead?"

"That's why we're here," said Clara, sharply. "Over time we've gathered things, knowledge; anything related to Silas and what he did. We think that it's possible to cut the cord between him and this world, but the only way is through a profound understanding of the occult – which we've been reluctant to employ until now."

They told me their plan – a plan so intricate it involved breaking back into the mansion, finding Silas Ashcroft's remains in some physical form or another and then performing an exorcism on the house to free it from his presence completely. Like Edgar pointed out: this thing was risky business; if any one of us went mad or died during such an affair… Well let's just say there weren't too many alternatives.

With my mind still filled by visions of suffering that could easily become reality if left unchecked; I agreed. For hours we worked tirelessly side by side collecting everything from herbs used in potions all the way down to weapons capable of defending ourselves against beings not entirely human anymore.

When evening fell upon us like a shroud over our heads -we found ourselves standing outside what looked like nothing less than pure evil personified as bricks joined together with mortar. The second my foot crossed its threshold however something strange happened: instead warmth welcoming me back into its embrace (like should have been) there was only ice-cold air prickling each hair on end as if warning them about danger soon to come…

We went inside anyways because armed knowledge hopelessness anyone can do almost anything they set their mind too.

CHAPTER 14:
The Perfect Storm

Inside the Ashcroft mansion, there was a feeling of impending doom that was almost tangible as we walked in. Darkness seemed to be alive and it swallowed our flashlights' beams of light and muffled the sound of our footsteps. We moved around quickly but silently because any action we took tonight could determine the rest of our lives.

Edgar led us through less-traveled hallways and secret doors using his knowledge of the house's layout he gained working here years ago when he was a kid. He always stayed away from main areas where the hand would show itself or other more dangerous entities were known to manifest themselves more aggressively. Mrs. Whitmore walked behind him closely, keeping everyone calm with her presence alone even though tensions ran high.

The deeper we went into this place, the thicker it became. Somehow, I felt like it knew what kind of night this was for it — that something terrible awaited us at its heart if only we could get there first! Whispers spoke words which vanished as soon as they were detected by my ears; however their maliciousness remained undoubted.

When we reached Silas Ashcroft's old personal study located at the mansion's core, things got colder inside both temperature-wise and emotionally speaking too – everything just felt wrong about being there now… The door leading into said room stood slightly ajar like an invitation into undoubtedly disastrous territory beyond those walls; Clara squeezed my shoulder gently before stepping past me through that entranceway.

The study itself occupied quite some space indeed featuring once splendid decor now fallen apart littered with dust everywhere one looked while many ancient forbidden knowledge-containing books lined up on shelves covering its walls; opposite wall held grotesque paintings portraying different dark rituals alongside hellish landscapes probably imagined by nobody else but Silas himself during his most disturbed moments – all these details together gave off strong vibes telling us loud and clear what needed to be done next!

Our lights started flickering as we began setting up for the ritual, casting eerie shadows upon moving parts of monstrous pictures hanging around us making everything there feel alive somehow... Edgar then proceeded to arrange artifacts brought here which were supposed to draw Silas out again before binding him back where he belonged.

As we did so, air turned heavy with a scent reminiscent of rotting flesh – physical representation left behind by the corrupted soul that belonged to none other than Ashcroft Senior! At this point whispers became more distinct forming into one voice unmistakably belonging to Silas himself; it seemed like he was having fun down there or wherever closer its origin could be located within these walls... "You can't catch what you don't comprehend" his mocking words echoed all over around accompanied by violent shaking.

"We know enough about you!" responded Edgar defiantly keeping calm despite increasing threats surrounding them both inside and outside their bodies; "And tonight is going to be your last night here!"

Clara started off the ceremony by chanting in some ancient language I'd never heard before but Mrs Whitmore joined her without hesitation and both women's voices sounded strange yet powerful together while also sounding familiar somehow ... The rest of us just looked at each other not knowing what else needed doing now until realization dawned upon me — relics! We had forgotten to place them around this room so that they could do their part too...

Silas's voice seemed to come from all around us, and his presence was so strong that it overwhelmed us as he fought against the bindings we were trying to make stronger. The earth shook beneath our feet, and the sound of breaking glass filled the air as the paintings on the walls shattered into fragments that cut our skin and made us bleed.

But still, we continued with the ritual: a single powerful force made up of many voices. With every word I felt him pulling at my soul – as if we were dragging him into this world to tie him down again; it was an incredible feeling of power mixed with fear.

Then just like that it stopped. The wind died down, and everything was quiet. For a moment there was nothing but ragged breaths in an empty room. We turned our lights back on slowly, shining them unsteadily through the dust-filled air.

The study was ruined; everything broken and torn apart from what had happened here tonight. But where Edgar had put that last relic in place – right in the middle of this room – there burned a small black mark on the floor: Silas had been bound once more.

And so we fell to pieces. Relief washed over us but also knowing it couldn't last forever: Silas' strength proved too great tonight when he overpowered all who stood against him. We were left alive only because we fought harder than ever before.

As we left that morning, the sun beginning its climb above trees in distance, I could feel something change with every step taken away from mansion walls. It was like house exhaling after holding its breath for too long – yet fight took much out of us still and each one knew how slow recovery would be while these shadows haunted us from within Ashcroft Manor.

We stayed outside for minute longer than needed – dawn air biting cold where inside suffocatingly hot – bodies beaten up spiritless but underneath fresh daylight glow there hung on something achieved even if fleeting. Edgar leaned against stone wall, pale face resolved against chill wind. “We did it,” he said to himself more than anyone else. “For now.”

“Yes,” Mrs Whitmore agreed with herself, voice carrying fears that hadn’t been spoken and battles never fought but won nonetheless – her eyes searching sky as if waiting for night to take shape and charge at us again. “But we cannot let our guard down… Silas digs deep into the world; these bonds may not hold forever.”

Clara turned back towards the house; dirt sweat blood smeared across her face telling tale of long fight spent in vain against impossible odds weariness blazed fierce defiance in eyes half-closed from exhaustion. “Not enough,” she said simply. “We have to keep watch, put up protections – this wasn’t victory, just another moment gained.”

A mixture of fear and determination had settled in me. Time has only been bought; Clara was right about that. We still needed to be eternally watchful, and the win would come when we find a way to sever Silas's link with this world forever, if possible.

We decided that we had to keep watch on the house every night. Edgar suggested that he looked into finding more permanent solutions by studying further those very old books we used to complement the ceremony since he knows much about magic from his studies in occultism. Mrs. Whitmore said she could offer her place as our base where we can meet up, plan things out and heal ourselves too if need be.

Getting ready to leave, I took one last look at the mansion. The sun was beginning its ascent towards evening thus illuminating those ancient bricks for the first time in years; their long shadows seemed to waver and twist as though they were being repelled by something within their own depths which acted like fear against light coming too close or seeing through it – maybe because this building has always been alive somehow but filled with negative energies over time until now when it might also resent our presence there.

Every step felt heavy that morning walking away from Ashcrofts' estate — not because physical wounds would take long before closing up but rather due mental ones whose darkness cast goes far beyond immediate perceptions, haunting forevermore at back parts of minds never silenced even by sleep itself.

When we returned back into Mrs. Whitmore's' abode again after having given some attention towards our injuries; cleaning cuts with antiseptics then covering them using sterile gauze pads fixed down securely beneath tapes applied gently yet skillfully so as not cause any discomfort or pain while removing later on either during dressing changes nor when changing dressings themselves – such care did soothe nerves somewhat though everyone understood very well indeed that these were only surface level scratches compared against deeper cuts made upon spirits & psyches which still needed more than just bandaging but some other kind of treatment as well.

Over strong cups filled up piping hot tea, plans for what should happen next began being laid out. The mood during this conversation was serious but not heavy; there was always an implied understanding among us all that what we were up against could never be allowed outside Willow's End – it had to stop here or else it would spread like wildfire across many other places too far from where most people live.

We ended the meeting by assigning tasks individually; Edgar would carry on conducting his researches into dark arts hoping discover ways strengthening our barriers even further. Clara took charge organizing shifts which were meant to keep watch over mansion round clock whilst also beginning work setting protective wards around its perimeter perhaps extending them throughout entire town if need be. Mrs Whitmore handled logistics side ensuring that The

Guardians remained well supplied thus enabling them continue keeping vigilance day in day out.

As far as I'm concerned though, personally speaking I felt obliged dig deeper into Ashcrofts' family history alongside that of their dwelling place itself — so many riddles still remain unsolved: Why did Silas fall so low down darkness path? Were there others before him or will there ever come another one after him? And lastly how do we make sure light wins against encroaching shadows once and for all?

Upon leaving Mrs Whitmores' house again now my mind had been made up about things; no matter what lay ahead along dangerous roads shrouded by foggy uncertainties — let alone battling such ancient malevolence until nothing else can dim skies over Willow's End with shade ever again… For me everything has only just started becoming clear at those very words armed knowledge, allies as well newfound determination surrounding safeguarding brightness midst gathering dusk eternally.

CHAPTER 15:

The Hand's Wrath

After a few days of peace, the tension had gone up so much more around Willow's End. The darkness kept growing thicker even though we tried our best and had put up Clara's protective wards all along the perimeter of town. It was almost like it was regrouping for another attack. The air felt heavy and charged – like the storm that was about to hit us overhead. If only we'd known it would break upon us so soon.

It started at a little inn one evening in Willow's End where people were gathered for their weekly trivia night. They were just trying to have some semblance of normalcy, but I guess part of me also hoped they might let something slip about how they were feeling or what they knew. Edgar and Clara flanked me; we were trying not to be noticed when the first sign hit. They should've taken it as an omen when the lights flickered – but for us, it was too familiar to be taken seriously anymore. Then, there was a sudden chill in the air (a totally unnatural one) and this wave of dread washed over me.

Whispers started running through the crowd as glasses began rattling on tables and this low rumble filled the room, darkening everyone's faces with fear. Panic broke out when people realized what was happening — I still get chills thinking about those next few seconds before shit got real bad — glass exploded inward from the front window of the bar, spraying everyone with shards as this severed hand came flying through it on some invisible force.

It landed on a table nearby with a sick thud and all hell broke loose as people scrambled over each other to get away from it.

The hand moved fast; quicker than anything its size should be able to move – at least that's how it seemed to my terrified brain at that moment. It skittered across the floor towards a man who was screaming and trying to crawl away from it, but before he could get very far the hand reached him. Its fingers wrapped around his ankle and tugged hard — there was this wet snapping noise, so loud over all the chaos – then another scream that cut off too soon.

I'll never forget how it looked: like an animal stalking its prey. It scuttled up tables and walls, its gnarled fingers curling around anything they could find. There was a woman who tripped in her panic to get away; she screamed when the hand caught her by the hair and dragged her across the floor. Her scalp stayed behind on the wood next to a pool of blood when it let go with one last jerk and twisted her neck around until something popped.

Everyone trampled each other trying to get out while Edgar, Clara and I tried to stop it. The only thing I remember about what Clara did is that she screamed incantations at it – stuff that usually slows them down for at least a little bit – except it didn't slow this hand down even for a second. Maybe Silas's wrath made it stronger or maybe there really was just more darkness in that house than any of us had realized.

It killed fast too; no messing around. Another person went down not five feet from us — an older guy who had been sitting at the bar nursing his beer since we got there. The hand lunged for him as he stumbled back into his stool after pushing himself up off the ground but missed getting hold of him on the way down. It must have been frustrated because instead of going back after him right away, it started slamming its palm onto random tables so hard they broke in half beneath its weight.

Edgar managed to corner it against one of these broken table halves with me backing him up; he wailed on it with an iron rod we'd brought along (supposedly weakens them) and for a second, I thought maybe we'd won. But then it screeched so loud I thought my ears would start bleeding and lunged at us twice as fast as before.

Just as I threw a vial of holy salt on top of it while it lunged at Edgar, its own body still struggling and twisting, the hand jerked when the salt touched it; steam erupted and another ear-splitting scream echoed throughout the room. We used this opportunity to drag back the hurt ones to safety; however, scorched and looking even more furious than before, the hand drew back for a moment before throwing itself again into battle.

The fight went on with Clara, Edgar and me teaming up against it as we tried moving out the remaining customers. It never seemed to tire or waver in its attacks either – everything about them showed an evil intent almost planned out step by step. In all this confusion Clara managed to cast a binding spell around its wrist while she was climbing one wall but her spell only slowed it down not holding forever which made way for Edgar's next punch knocking the hand into fireplace where flames appeared to swallow it.

For a second there we thought maybe we got rid of that thing; fire consumed what remained from cursed flesh. But no sooner had our eyes dart towards charred shapeless mass when burnt remains start pulling themselves together again forming familiar wicked silhouette.

The night finished off with destroyed inn, shocked community and three tired disillusioned individuals. Hand disappeared into darkness leaving behind ruined town scared more than ever before said attack is sign Silas still has power over us.

As last wounded were being loaded onto ambulances at dawn after night filled with screams that seemed never ending so did realization how badly we screwed up hit us like sledgehammer. The hand was still out there somewhere waiting knowing now that anytime anywhere can be next. What happened at inn served as brutal reminder showing just how weak and powerless really are against enemy like this.

Sitting amid destroyed inn watching sun come up alongside Clara and Edgar knew battle had just begun but now stakes risen higher than ever – dealing with not just incredibly vicious but also highly intelligent being capable of planning carrying out attacks down to last detail.

“We need regroup and think up new plan,” Edgar said grimly surveying damage his face etched with exhaustion and determination, “This wasn’t just an attack; it was statement. Silas isn’t defending himself – he’s declaring war.”

Clara nodded her eyes were bloodshot from lack of sleep but burned brighter than ever before. “We underestimated him” she admitted pulling jacket tighter around herself against morning cold, “My wards spells obviously won’t work now. We need something stronger… Something that lasts.”

Smoke mingled with smell blood underneath our noses as bodies continued getting loaded into ambulances around us making sure nobody left behind after such long night. What used be cozy little inn where travelers could find rest warmth laughter now resembled battle ground stained forever ghostly imprints supernatural anger upon its walls.

While emergency officials finished clearing the area and attending to casualties, our small group crowded together, pretending to be a war council of sorts against an enemy we could not see. It was decided that we should go back to Mrs. Whitmore's house; it was the only place left where we could feel safe and normal.

Once inside, surrounded by the ancient texts and artifacts that filled her home, we threw ourselves into research with more fervor than before. We knew what we had to do: find a way not just to bind Silas but banish him from this world forever. To achieve this would involve delving deeper into the dark arts than any of us cared for, but tonight had proven that half-measures were no longer enough.

In between searching through dusty grimoires and consulting translations of obscure manuscripts, we discovered the potential for a stronger ritual – one that might sever Silas's connection with our reality once and for all. The ritual would be dangerous; it would require components hard to come by and jeopardize our very souls – but what other choice did we have? If left unchecked, Silas would continue wreaking havoc on everything around him.

We went out every day gathering supplies while fortifying Mrs. Whitmore's house with protective spells and wards known to fight off any entity attracted by such provocation as ours in this weakened state — turning it into something more akin now to a fortress than anything else. Each night became a waiting game: Would he strike again before we were ready?

Finally, after days of preparation fueled by caffeine alone, there came an evening when all signs pointed toward go-time. The new ritual had been set for next full moon – less than 48 hours away at this point – when veil between worlds is said to thin most dramatically… so if ever there was going be chance success then surely it must come now! We gathered at edge Ashcroft property which seemed outside range some dark energy emitting from within mansion itself.

As soon as that silver light touched the ground, we began. The world around us seemed to crackle with potential; every word of our incantation carried weight beyond measure. Soil shook beneath our feet, wind screamed in our ears, and deep within those rotting walls something stirred restlessly.

This time we were not just defenders anymore; this time we were aggressors – fighting back against an unseen enemy who had taken too much already. Our working reached its crescendo: either it would cleanse world or destroy everything.

And then… nothing. It was as if all sound had been sucked out universe, leaving behind only an expectant silence. We waited there for what felt like forever: still, silent waiting – hearts pounding against ribcages – for any indication that what we'd done might actually work.

In end result of that night's ritual – whether victory or another nightmare escalation (which by this point felt almost more fitting) in our ongoing war against Silas – would make itself apparent over time. But one thing remained certain even now: we had crossed line tonight which could never be uncrossed again. The fight for Willow's End had entered new phase altogether, and sitting on outskirts it readying ourselves face whatever came next seemed lone option available to us at present.

CHAPTER 16:

Facing The Past

After our rite, silence fell like a ghost on us in the dark. We hardly breathed. The air was alive somehow, charged — there was some kind of tension in it that felt almost solid. Gradually that sense of immediate threat ebbed away; the night took back over its usual peace broken only by distant cries and a little soft wind stirring the trees.

We kept watch, scanning shadows, waiting for — expecting — another hand to reach out toward us or some new horror to show itself. But as minutes turned into hours without incident we began to let ourselves relax a little. It was Edgar who spoke first; his voice was low and tired.

"It's done," he said, still staring toward the Ashcroft house. "For now, anyway. But we need to keep an eye out; we've stirred things up too much for Silas not to react."

Clara nodded; her face was white in the moonlight and her eyes shone hard with determination. “We’ll take shifts keeping watch on the mansion and everything around it,” she said quietly. “This isn’t over.”

While we walked back to Mrs. Whitmore’s house what had happened began to sink in: this ritual hadn’t been about protecting us from something or tying something down so it couldn’t move — it’d been an attack against Silas Ashcroft himself, an attempt at cutting through whatever thin threads still held him here among us living people. Whether that meant he would be gone once and for all after tonight or just take more drastic revenge I didn’t know.

Mrs. Whitmore made us a late meal when we got back — her way of bringing us back down to earth after dealing with so much unearthly stuff all night long — and while we ate our talk turned toward Silas Ashcroft’s history and where his dark legacy came from in Willow’s End. She’d lived here all her life; these were stories handed down to her.

“He was always a little different, even before he started messing around with black magic,” she said softly in the quiet kitchen. “His family had money, power — they could do anything they wanted in this town. But Silas wasn’t like them. He was interested in old books, forbidden knowledge.”

Something faraway came into Mrs. Whitmore's eyes as she remembered what she'd heard when she was young. "They say he lost somebody he loved very much — his wife, Lydia. People do desperate things when they're grieving, and that's what happened to Silas: grief drove him to necromancy. He thought he could bring her back, or at least…well, you know."

That put a new spin on our enemy's malevolence — it made me think about how darkness often grew out of pain and loss; the tragedy of Silas's story served as a kind of explanation for why he had tried so hard not to die once upon a time (and failed).

Sitting in the lounge's dim light with only the soft ticking of the clock to keep me company, I couldn't help but think about how hauntingly beautiful our fight was. There is something tragically poetic about going up against a ghost; not just any ghost, mind you, but one that represents a troubled past filled with pain and suffering. It felt like we weren't battling Silas Ashcroft alone – it was as if we were also grappling with all of humanity's sorrows that had brought about his curse.

The silence was broken by a sudden burst of static from the walkie-talkie on the table beside me, followed by Clara's voice – low and tense. "Movement at the manor," she said. "Something's happening."

I sprung into action, snatching up my flashlight and the walkie-talkie before charging out into the cold night.

The journey to the mansion was surreal. The moon hung high overhead, casting long shadows that seemed to dance and sway with every gust of wind. As I drew nearer, I noticed lights – candles, perhaps – flickering in and out of existence behind its many windows; they appeared like breaths being drawn in through pale lips.

When I reached its gate, Clara was waiting for me just beyond its threshold. Her face looked pinched beneath her thick coat; her eyes were wide with fear and excitement alike.

"This time is different," she whispered hoarsely as I approached her side. "Can't you feel it? The air… it's electric."

We stood there together for what must have been several minutes or hours – time itself seemed susceptible to whatever strange forces were at play within those walls – before eventually tearing our gazes away from one another and back toward the house.

It pulsed in front of us: an ancient heart awakened after centuries spent sleeping beneath layers upon layers of earth and mortar; a beast roused from slumber; a tomb caught in the act of unbecoming. And, just then, staring into that shifting sea of candlelight… it was impossible to deny how very much alive Silas Ashcroft still was.

So we stood there, Clara and I – heartbeats pounding like war drums in our ears – and we knew that this night would not be like any other before it.

"Not yet," Silas whispered through the trees that surrounded us now. "Not yet…"

CHAPTER 17:
Fall Of Darkness

The mansion's eyes, flickering through windows like a predator's in the dark, were attentive. With fear and determination, we moved towards it with cautious steps on the wet ground, as she had said the atmosphere was electric; malevolent energy seemed to emanate from every wall of Ashcroft's house.

The door groaned opened itself when we reached the front entrance—an invitation to enter into the heart of darkness. Taking a deep breath, we went in; our torches carving thin tracks through stuffy darkness along the great hall.

It was worse inside than I remembered. The shadows were thicker here—almost tangible—clinging to every object and corner as if it were an oppressive sheet of cloth. The air was cold; much colder than outside that night, carrying with it a smell that could only be described as rottenness mingled with something else… something unnatural.

We proceeded slowly. Our footsteps echoed loudly within this unnatural silence that clung over everything within these haunted walls. A soft dragging came from above us as we passed by the grand staircase—a shiver ran down my spine: I could still vividly recall how those hands had attacked me violently just days ago.

When we arrived at where Silas' presence had last been felt—the study—the door swung open wide with a groan revealing its deranged state: books lay scattered about while papers covered every inch of floor space; burnt wax filled the air alongside stale odors left behind by long-extinguished candles which had not been replaced for years perhaps—centuries even! It felt like such rooms hung heavy upon themselves waiting for someone else to disturb them once more…

Her face impassive, Clara began chanting some protection spell under her breath whilst looking around warily—for good reason too given what lurked in this place… Though uttered Guardians ancient tongue these words vibrated throughout surrounding atmosphere creating ripples that pushed against the dark temporarily enabling us to keep moving farther into mansion towards cellar where Silas made his most sinister experiments.

The door to the cellar stood slightly ajar; an eerie silence fell upon us as we descended its creaking steps. Down there it was pitch-black, so much so that our torch beams seemed swallowed by infinite nothingness.

At the foot of those same stairs lay before me a vast chamber filled with shadows which receded further back than eye could see; here also appeared cooler air though still damp and earthy but mixed this time with something far fouler—a sickly sweet stench reminiscent perhaps more closely associated with rotting flesh than mere death itself.

We had to tread carefully due unevennesses in floor underfoot caused by all manner of junk scattered about within these depths such as pieces broken furniture but above all else chains—chains hanging from ceiling or lining walls were what really unnerved me because they spoke volumes regarding what kind things Silas must have done down here!

As we progressed deeper into this cramped space so too did its boundaries seem close in upon us until finally emerging amidst darkness there loomed before our eyes an odd-shaped figure stooped over like some deformed semi-human silhouette against blackened backdrop… It was Silas—what remained him bound up together creation he'd made (the severed hand) life-force still linked between two.

It was a hideous sight: his body rotten bits mummified others grotesquely preserved while only one thing about him seemed alive—his eyes burning fiercely red lights fixed directly onto both Clara and I whose approach clearly had not gone unnoticed!

Whispering a warning, Clara's voice barely carried. "Be ready. He knows we're here."

Silas stirred at the sound, chains rattling softly. A growl came out of him, deep and furious. Then he lunged violently towards us with a sudden motion, held back by the chains that rang as they strained.

The next few moments were a whirl of motion and fear. Silas attacked like a madman; his fingers had stretched into long claws that reached for us with unexpected strength. Clara fought back with spells, her voice rising above the cries of Silas, while I tried to find a way to put an end to him.

It was a brutal battle: Silas caught my arm at one point, his grip freezing and tight. His skin on mine felt like death itself brushing against me and I screamed not only from pain but also because it horrified me so much that I had made contact with something entirely corrupt.

With all my might I pulled away leaving some of my flesh behind in his hand — seeing this made Clara redouble her efforts; her spells wrapped more tightly around Silas as we readied ourselves for the final incantation which would sever his ties with this world forever.

Both of our voices were necessary for the incantation which turned them into one powerful chant filling up every inch of space within those cellar walls shaking foundations of that mansion even though it seemed impossible considering how loud they were already due to screaming coming from downstairs where all these years ago another boy went missing without trace… Silas writhed under its weight crying out in pain mixed with anger because nothing could have prepared him or anyone else there tonight.

But we did not give up – instead kept chanting pouring everything into those words until at last he fell down lifeless screaming ceased spirits having gone away forevermore after what seemed an eternity but probably took only seconds before everything became silent once again except for heavy breathing.

We stood still there for a while panting covered in sweat and dirt realizing what just happened and how much it cost us. We fought the darkest part of Silas Ashcroft and won, yet our scars will forever remind us about that day.

When we were going up stairs from basement to outside through small door leading into kitchen because you couldn't use main entrance at night without anyone knowing who went where or when – anyway as soon as I saw daylight streaming down those steps ahead of me like some kind welcoming committee after long journey through hell itself… well let's just say things started looking up then.

CHAPTER 18:

The Last Casualty

The sunrise that succeeded our stand-off in the cellar did nothing to soothe. The house was quiet – a silent witness of old terrors – its corners darker and more foreboding than ever in the pale light. Our footsteps echoed as Clara and I walked through empty halls, each one tolling like a bell marking the hollowness we had come up against.

We split up, planning to cover more ground by checking the mansion for residual malevolence or any other victims left behind by Silas's darkness. Clara took the upper floors, her determination palpable like the silence between us. I moved back down into the bowels of the house, drawn irresistibly once again to the basement where Silas had been last seen.

The air grew colder as I descended; dirt and rot mixed with something else — something metallic and keen. Blood. Realizing it quickened my pulse, sharpening my awareness as I went lower still. The flashlight's dim beam began to flicker, casting unsettling shades on walls that seemed to throb with an inner dark.

In reaching the basement itself, there could be no doubt about what caused such a smell. A figure lay crumpled on the floor at its center, surrounded by a wide halo of dark liquid. My heart dropped. Not another person lost! But when I approached closer with my light source trained ahead…Michael's throat had been cut almost all way through; his would-be head dangled off as though only loosely attached — edges jaggedly gaping apart against their own gloom while silently screaming at me from under those sickly beams overhead.

I knelt beside him, hands shaking too much for usefulness yet still searching out futile signs of existence; vacant eyes stared upwards into emptiness beyond all reflection or reason now sought after so desperately before getting snuffed away entirely forevermore here tonight once again anyhow somehow somewhere such as this place—this house! That he had returned here at all just to die…It made me sick inside my stomach. After everything else that must have been seen through before survival even became an option once more – still some part of him must have felt drawn back by unfinished business or lingering connection perhaps?

Guilt welled up inside alongside anger: How could we think banishment complete? Was there something more left uncut, undrawn? Or had the hand gone mad independent from its master's will altogether and become a savage force on its own with other violent ends in mind?

It was brutal. Michael's hands clenched into fists so tight they drew blood from his own palms; desperation showed through those deep wounds where strength failed to answer back against invisible assailant somewhere out there who chose not play fair but instead took cowardly shots lying low waiting until victim least expected then striking hard like lightning bolt from blackened heavens above while struggling gasping clawing writhing screaming — tearing room apart furniture flying papers scattered glass broken lightbulbs shattered all around.

I straightened my posture, determination crystalizing within me. This has got to stop right now. No more dying; no more shadows. Everything else lurking upstairs claims life after life – I can't let it happen anymore. Taking one last calming breath, I turned away from basement and went off searching for Clara

I agreed by nodding my head. It was a last resort but we had to do it. We couldn't risk any more lives nor could we let the mansion remain as a beacon for more darkness.

So we moved fast, taking things that would burn from all over the house — old papers, curtains, anything that would catch fire easily. We set them up in piles throughout the rooms.

When everything was in place, we stood together at the entrance of the mansion and looked back at those black halls where so much terror had taken place. Then, with a glance between us, I lit the first torch and threw it onto one of the piles.

It caught quickly — the materials were dry and hungry for flames. They spread up curtains and leapt from book to book on shelves. Smoke billowed everywhere then, black and thick with an acrid smell clinging to it; but underneath there was something else — beneath all that smoke was a sense of purification; it felt like the fire was cleansing not only this house but also our town's air of its long history with evil.

The mansion burned fiercely around us; heat beat against our faces and singed our eyes. Night settled back into silence outside except for distant night-creature calls plus crackling fire sounds near us.It really was over this time.The Ashcroft mansion would be reduced to ashes which meant no more darkness could ever sprout out again through its doors into Willow's End or anywhere else.

Clara and I turned away when roof caved in over flames' highest reach each other's faces dirty tears streaming down knowing what came next what always came after this stuff happened haunted sleepless nights agony regret forever etched behind eyelids dead friends missing people doomed memories unspeakable horrors witnessed countless times before But still somehow someway kind of nice feeling too even though you knew better than think like that because if you did then there'd always have been something wrong with you or something else off balance in the world like maybe there had to be some other way of looking at all this so it didn't seem quite so senselessly random as everything sometimes did seem but there never was and we both knew it only too well.

As we walked past the burning building, the sky started getting light with dawn. The air was fresher, cleaner — it felt almost like the smoke had burned away more than just Silas Ashcroft's physical legacy; like maybe that fire finally killed whatever he left behind here in Willow's End too.

“We should keep an eye on things,” Clara said, her voice raspy from smoke and crying. “Make sure nothing survives. No relics, no pieces that could bring back the darkness.”

I nodded my agreement but my mind is heavy with thoughts as we walk away from each other towards where everyone else is waiting for us: “Yeah… set up shifts with others…” I tried to say more but couldn't find words strong enough so instead I let silence fill space around us knowing full well why she did what she'd done how much worse it would have been if not for her sacrifices our vigilance the last duty owed those who suffered.

Sunrise painted clouds orange pink over Mrs Whitmore's house where we found her standing outside waiting for us. Her face looked one part relieved one part sad as she took in our smoke-streaked skin and heavy shoulders.

“You did it then?” She asked, voice shaking slightly.

“We did,” I tell her firmly even though all feel is bone-deep tiredness right now. “It’s over Mrs Whitmore. The mansion can’t hurt anyone ever again.”

She nods, tears brimming over eyes that haven't seen such terrible things since childhood pulled into a gentle hug against time-wrinkled chest. “Thank you.” Her voice breaks up around those two words but I hear enough of them anyway: “For everything.”

The period that came after this was time for rest and thinking. The town slowly recovered however it didn’t completely heal from the tragedy. Different families cried for their dear ones and the community united to assist those who were hurt by the event. The place where the big house was situated had been put under close watch. Nevertheless, all that remained there were ashes together with burned woods. Amongst the ruins ,nothing moved, no shades flickered right at the periphery of one’s sight . It was really finished .

To avoid any further unpleasant surprises in different regions of the globe in days to come, Clara with me as well as other members of The Guardians continued meeting frequently so that we could talk over what happened during our missions and share knowledge gained from those undertakings . However, currently nothing threatened Willow's End.

In this month which transformed into months bringing about weeks then life got a new beat . Together with it healing took place both within ourselves and around us but still those moments when everything seemed hopeless remained engraved in my memory just like they did in every person's mind living there then . We kept communication open among ourselves knowing very well that such bonds are created during hard times hence can never be broken.

It was one evening when I sat on top of a hill looking down upon town from where mansion once stood; I started meditating about this journey! Yes indeed fear ,pain ,and despair were part of it but they worked hand in glove with faith ,hope love which made our hearts stronger than ever before thus enabling us face darkness head on without flinching.The wind blew harder rustling leaves through trees causing me think that whispers voices carried by breezes might be real or figments imaginary . But alas! I couldn't believe my ears because just then everything went silent leaving behind nothing save for sound made by falling leaflets. And instantly i managed crack a smile filled with exhaustion yet joy while shifting focus towards twinkling stars.

This knowledge would be remembered by Willow's End as well as myself; however, we had no option rather than moving onwards bearing torch against blackness which acted such that it became illumination during our teenage years living among shadows. For now, that's all.

CHAPTER 19:

The Ceremony

While the city of Willow's End found its way back to normalcy little by little, the memories about what had happened at the Ashcroft mansion were still alive in the minds and hearts of all those who were affected. Peace eluded me — every time I closed my eyes, I saw again all those terrible nights one after another like pictures in a madman's flip book.

In a late autumn afternoon like that, when I walked through our now empty town and leaves whispered as they rustled under my feet chillingly, I knew where I wanted to go: it was an old cemetery in town. A place of silence where people can think about things quietly.

When I got there, among many graves which did not bear the name 'Ashcroft' but still held themselves responsible for everything that had happened at that haunted house, stood Michael's tombstone — he was just a handyman whose life was taken away by the same evil we fought so hard against. Looking down on his resting place, it occurred to me how heavy this victory is if you have lost so much on your way.

I must admit that while standing there thinking about him alone with myself, somebody gently touched my shoulder from behind which made me frightened. It turned out to be Clara who brought peace simply being here with us. She always finds these places of sorrows too.

"We did what we could," she said softly reading through my eyes "but... but it costed too much."

I nodded trying to swallow words before speaking them out loud "Too high for some." My gaze returned onto grave again "How can we come into terms with this Clara? How do you live with choices?"

Her eyes met mine looking solemnly deep into each other 's souls as if asking more questions than answering anything at all. "We keep them alive in our memories," she replied still staring into space without breaking eye contact at any moment "and fight back dark forces in their names. That's all we can do."

Her words struck me as simple truth giving peace where it could have never been found otherwise. We stayed silent for a while longer paying respect not only to Michael but also every single person who suffered because of that haunted house on the hill.

As the sun began to set behind great trees surrounding cemetery many things started getting darker around us until we were left alone with long shadows cast by tombstones between them making everything seem unreal or scary even though it was still day time ... But then again — isn't peace always fragile? Darkness has infinite patience, I know better than anyone else does.

One cold night while I was coming back home after meeting with the Guardians, an old Ashcroft property caught my attention. A slight glow from it appeared before me. My heart sank; even though the evil which had infected its soil for ages was destroyed along with the mansion itself but not completely.

Promptly, I moved towards the gleam, growing more scared with each step. It turned out to be no fire's flicker but rather a something ethereal – a spectral presence that sent shivers down my spine.

There stood what used to be Silas Ashcroft in middle of where once his house stood dilapidated by time – only now he appeared see-through and radiant with otherworldly light, still bound to this earth as if his curse hadn't been completely broken by us.

Silas' ghost looked at me then; his eyes were empty yet ablaze with unabated hatred. He mouthed words and though they didn't reach my ears I knew them well enough: he hadn't finished with Willow's End yet.

It hit like lightning – we were not done fighting. We'd just changed tactics.

So I took a deep breath, held onto myself and met its stare boldly having seen too much already to be frightened easily anymore. "You can't scare me, "I murmured through teeth clenched against icy wind blowing around us both; those words were meant more for myself than anything else at that moment in time.

The apparition began fading away slowly as if dissolving into thin air together with its shine melting away like morning mist under rising sunrays; however this encounter served as stern warning that darkness still hung overhead and would continue doing so until Kingdom Come thus making necessary perpetual watchfulness our duty hereafter.

Realizing this fact on my way back home where weight of ongoing struggle pressed heavily upon shoulders , it became clear that any respite found had been nothing but brief lull before next storm; still we were ready having been tested by life too often not to be and standing together united against common foe – Willow's End shall never sleep again whiles I am alive for it is my place keep an eye out of what lurks in shadows lest they devour all light.

CHAPTER 20:

Repeats Of History

The phantom figure of Silas Ashcroft sat in the mind like a nightmare that would not fade with the morning. It was a reminder that some fights never end; they just change shape and wait for another opportunity to attack. I hardened my resolve – Willow's End would not fall into darkness again while I still drew breath.

In the weeks after Silas' ghost confronted me, I delved deeper into the history of the Ashcroft family, looking for anything that could give us an advantage if the spirit tried to reassert its influence. The local library became my second home, its musty archives containing years of forgotten whispers.

On a rainy afternoon as I pored over old newspaper clippings and personal journals from people who had lived during Silas' time, one diary caught my eye – a woman who had been a maid at the mansion.

Her entries shed chilling light on the daily terrors that occurred behind those walls under Silas' reign.

The diary was old; its pages were yellowed and brittle, but the handwriting was still legible. With each page, she described her growing horror at Silas' rituals, her fellow servants vanishing and the strange sounds that echoed through the house at night. Her words painted a picture of a man consumed by grief and twisted obsession; his humanity eroded by his flirtations with dark forces.

One entry in particular stood out – it was a detailed account of a ritual gone awry. Hidden in shadows, she watched as Silas attempted to summon something from beyond the veil. The entity he called broke free of his control, wreaked havoc in the mansion and killed three people before it could be banished.

The description of the entity itself and elements of ritual used were disturbingly graphic – thick smell of iron and fear clogged air around it, while writhing shadows with eyes like burning coals best approximated its appearance. Servant's account included sketches of Silas' sigils which I copied down carefully, hoping they might help us shore up our defences against him.

Armed with this new information, I met Clara and Edgar to compare notes. We pored over the sketches and diary entries, each feeling a mix of dread and resolve. Edgar suggested using the sigils as a basis for new wards, adapting them to cage rather than summon.

“We can turn Silas’ own tools against him,” he said, his eyes shining with an unpleasant kind of excitement. “Reconfigure the sigils so they trap and suppress his spirit if he tries to manifest again.”

Clara nodded grimly in agreement. “We’ll need to do the ritual at the mansion’s ruins – fortify the very ground against his return. It’s going to be risky but I think it’s our best shot.”

We started getting ready for it. We collected stuff, repeated the spells and studied the signs until we knew them by heart. Everything was done quickly but with care as if Silas could see us at any moment and try to stop what we were doing.

And then came the night of our counter-ritual. It felt like the air itself had held its breath when we set up in the ruins of that old house, with just a sliver of a moon hanging over us so that most of our circle was left in darkness except for where it touched the broken foundations and charred remains. We took our places – Clara across from Edgar across from me, with the sigils drawn into the earth forming a protective wall around each of us.

Clara started speaking, and as soon as she did there was this cold wind that seemed to come out of nowhere but down from above, out of that black sky. Edgar and I joined her, and it was like all three voices became one: powerful words spoken with power. The sigils began to glow softly at first – just a pale light – but they got brighter and brighter as we put more and more energy into what we were doing.

Then, right in front of us – right in the middle of our circle – everything sort of rippled like water does when you throw a stone into its stillness… only this ripple came with a sound like thunder. There stood Silas's spirit or whatever it was: flickering in shape but solid enough to see he wasn't happy; his face twisted up into some kind of silent scream or roar or something. The sigils flared even brighter than they'd been before he showed up, and his figure looked almost like it'd been pressed flat against some invisible barrier which kept trying to give way under him.

He fought hard. You could feel it: this force pushing against ours; dark waves rolling through space itself. But we fought back too, and louder than ever – driving him away from us; keeping him within the bounds we'd set for him.

By the time dawn was about to break he had become so faint that you could almost see through him and his anger was nothing more than a weak echo trapped inside our defenses. And then at last he just vanished, like a light going out or smoke dissipating into air – only once more the sigils flared up bright one final time before they faded back down into earth where they'd come from.

We were all of us completely drained, but it didn't matter: we'd won again. It couldn't stay quiet here forever, but for now Willow's End was safe. We turned its own shadow against itself this time around – and in doing that found one another's strength as well: forged together by dangers shared and overcome.

CHAPTER 21:
Willow's End Ashes

The sunrise over Willow's End the next morning after our ceremony was fresh and cloudless, the sky cleansed of the oppressive weight that had clung like a portent. Standing among the rubble of what used to be the Ashcroft mansion, now only a memory and a warning, I felt that something was different. The fight we had wasn't just another battle; it was a turning point for this town, for every one of us who stood against the dark.

Willow's End started to heal in those weeks following. People heard about Silas Ashcroft's ghost and our final confrontation not just within town but beyond its borders as well — curiosity brought visitors looking for proof of the paranormal. But there were no malevolent spirits here, no dark energies; only a community coming together again after being tested so hard.

Still, some wounds didn't show on the skin. The physical damage got fixed up easily enough, but we kept those lost to Silas' legacy alive in quiet moments and solemn remembrances. In the center of town we put up a memorial — simple but powerful, like everything else that saved our peace.

For me personally, fighting Silas became part of my identity. I spent days working on repairs and nights walking around making sure wards held tight across all corners. Originally made up mostly by locals with strong wills – Guardians had grown into something much bigger than themselves over time; now training others against supernatural threats should they ever return here.

One evening while sunset painted everything red Clara joined Edgar and myself at said memorial where we stood silently until she spoke first into silence "Did we?" her voice barely audible yet filled with so many emotions unspoken.

"We did…" He responded softer usual stoicism washed warm sunlight "…but it had high price."

"Yes…" My words carried Doris presence fear choices losses "…Yet future has been secured for Willow's End, when it seemed like there was none. That must count for something."

"It does," Clara nodded slowly agreement "And it always will. We'll make sure of that."

From where we'd been standing now planning next moves – how best shield town magically from evil; educate younger generation about supernatural realities – I could see clearly our roles as protectors had only just begun if anything they'd grown bigger.

When the night arrived we left memorial behind walking through quiet empty streets which now belonged entirely to night but also joy and laughter. The fear that once smothered this place was gone forever replaced with lights twinkling through windows music carrying on breeze signs life once overshadowed itself by

We stopped at edge town looking back towards silhouette against dark sky "Will this ever truly end?" Clara's voice trembled slightly.

"In some ways, no," I told them honestly. "But that is why we are here. To watch, to protect. We have learned so much and will use it to keep the dark at bay. Not just this place, but any place it may rise."

They nodded; they understood the truth in those words. Our peace had come at a price — a commitment born from trial.

On our way back home, the stars above were bright as ever, their constellations indifferent to mortal concerns. It was under their timeless gaze that I found my purpose rekindled. Willow's End was more than a town; it was a monument to human resilience, to our capacity for bravery and selflessness when confronted with unfathomable shadows.

The shadows could never be fully eradicated, but so long as there were those who fought against them — who stood up and said no to the night — there would always be hope. And in Willow's End, hope was something we cherished; it was a beacon that would see us through any storm.

As this chapter of our lives neared its end, I knew one thing beyond all doubt: we were prepared for whatever came next.

CONCERNING

Bennard Terrell

A traveler who loves to write, Bennard Terrell is a writer. He takes his readers on unimaginable trips. He has always been able to captivate his audience by telling stories with interesting structures.

His writings reflect a fully lived and keenly observed life; thus, they are a mosaic of experiences mirrored through different characters and places. Anthropology being an area of specialization for Bennard, he studied it globally which explains why realistic cultural representations as well as deep-seated human realities have found their way into his novels.

Each new release should not only tell but also ignite people's own questions while leading them to self-discovery through literature says Bennard Terrel . It is through this mysterious aspect around our being that loves shines in all his narratives delivered through beautiful words that can be understood by anybody anywhere without excluding anybody hence some might argue that we do not just read but live them.

One must be ready to enter completely alien or entirely familiar surroundings when going from one page to another of this recently published book because according to him every single piece of work constitutes nothing else than communication between writers themselves and readers like us; even more so if such authors write sincerely hoping their words touch us deeply somewhere inside our hearts where feelings forever reside until death does part these two souls bound together for eternity too if necessary…

To stay posted with what Bennard Terrell is working on next, where he will be reading or anything else visit www.bennardterrell.com.

www.ingramcontent.com/pod-product-compliance
Lightning Source LLC
LaVergne TN
LVHW010110170826
845678LV00012B/2333

* 9 7 8 2 4 6 5 6 4 1 3 7 0 *